# G

## Cozy Mystery Series Book 15

# **Hope Callaghan**





---

**Visit my website for new releases and special offers: hopecallaghan.com**

Thank you, Peggy H., Cindi G., Barbara W. and Wanda D. for taking the time to preview *Greed with Envy,* for the extra sets of eyes and for catching all my mistakes.

A special thanks to my reader review team: Alice, Amary, Barbara, Becky, Becky B, Brinda, Cassie, Christina, Debbie, Denota, Devan, Francine, Grace, Jan, Jo-Ann, Joeline, Joyce, Jean K., Jean M., Kathy, Lynne, Megan, Melda, Kat, Linda, Lynne, Pat, Patsy, Paula, Renate, Rita, Rita P, Shelba, Tamara and Vicki.

# Table of Contents

# Like Free Books?

Get Free & Discounted Books, Giveaways & New Releases When You Subscribe To My Free Cozy Mysteries Newsletter!

**hopecallaghan.com/newsletter**

# Chapter 1

"Grams." Ryan Adams tugged on the sleeve of his grandmother's silk blouse. "What does eloped mean?" he whispered.

Gloria lowered her head. "Eloped means to sneak off and get married."

Ryan's eyes widened. "You mean Andrea didn't have permission to get married?"

Gloria grinned. "Yes. She had permission. It's just that Brian and she decided it would be more fun to sneak off and get married." It was a simple answer to a complicated situation.

Brian Sellers and Andrea Malone, Gloria's friends, had gone through several difficult months, starting with Brian's amnesia, some misunderstandings between the couple and more recently, Andrea's escape to the island of

Nantucket where she met her parents and another unexpected guest.

Things had deteriorated when the ex-boyfriend was found dead and Brian was under suspicion for his murder. Gloria couldn't blame the couple for eloping. In fact, she might have done the same thing had she been in their shoes.

After sneaking off to Niagara Falls, the excited newlyweds returned home, promising to renew their vows in front of family and friends, which is what they were doing now.

The *Wedding March* began to play. "Here she comes." Gloria stood. Ryan, along with his older brother, Tyler, and Paul, Gloria's husband, followed suit.

Sudden tears sprang to Gloria's eyes as she watched a radiant Andrea slowly walk down the aisle. David Thornton, Andrea's father, smiled proudly as he accompanied his daughter to the front of the Church of God where Brian, decked out in a snazzy three-piece suit, and Pastor Nate stood waiting.

After the bride and her father reached the front, the guests inside the packed sanctuary sat. Many of the faces were familiar, but there were a few Gloria didn't recognize.

The ceremony was short and sweet, and when Pastor Nate informed Brian he could kiss his bride, the guests jumped to their feet and began applauding. No one applauded louder than Gloria did and she beamed with pride. Andrea was like a second daughter to her and she liked to think she had a small hand in matchmaking.

While guests stayed behind to congratulate the couple, Gloria and her grandsons hurried to her car, while Paul, who had driven separately, headed to his vehicle.

Gloria and her friends Dot, Lucy, Rose and Ruth were in charge of the reception, which was being held at *Magnolia Mansion,* Andrea's spacious home or "mini mansion" atop a hill not far from Lake Terrace.

Dot and Rose, co-owners of Dot's Restaurant in downtown Belhaven, were handling the catering. Lucy and Ruth were in charge of decorating and entertainment and Gloria, the Mistress of Ceremonies, was in charge of overseeing everything.

When Gloria, Ryan and Tyler reached Andrea's place, Dot and Rose were already up to their elbows in hors d'oeuvres.

"How did it go?" Dot glanced up from a large tray of canapés.

"It was boring." Tyler reached for a treat and Gloria tapped the top of his hand. "Uh-uh. We have to wait to eat."

"You should have taken a few moments off and gone with us." Gloria turned to face Dot. "This all could've waited."

"Oh I dunno about that Gloria." Rose wiped her hands on the front of her apron. "We got a hot mess going on in here."

"Let me help." Gloria reached for an apron, hanging on a hook by the door and turned to her grandsons. "Why don't you take Brutus out for a walk before the guests arrive?" Brutus was Andrea's black Labrador retriever.

The boys, who were staying with Gloria overnight so that Gloria's daughter, Jill, and her husband could enjoy a quick weekend getaway alone, headed out.

Gloria turned her attention to the task at hand. "What can I do?"

Dot handed her a bag of crusty bread slices and a large bowl of tomato concoction. "You can assemble the bruschetta. Was Margaret there?"

Margaret Hansen was one of the women's close friends and a resident of Belhaven.

Gloria untied the bag of bread. "No, now that you mention it. I need to call her. I wonder if Don and she are going to try to make it to the reception."

Don, Margaret's husband, had recently suffered a heart attack and since coming home from the hospital had required almost around the clock care.

From what Margaret had told her friends, Don had gotten into a heated argument on the golf course with another member of Montbay Hills Golf and Country Club. Don collapsed on the green and they'd called an ambulance.

Margaret was responsible for the brunt of his care but the other girls had taken turns sitting with Don so Margaret could take small breaks. Don appeared to be on the mend, so much so that the couple was bickering. Stir crazy is what Gloria called it. Don wasn't used to being confined to the house and Margaret wasn't used to having him underfoot.

“Hopefully she’ll be able to stop by for a few minutes,” Gloria said. “After I finish here, I’ll run by there to give her a break.”

The trio finished assembling the appetizers and arranging them on the tables in the front hall where the cocktail reception was being held.

Dot and Rose began the dinner preparation at the same time Ray, Dot’s husband, and Johnnie, Rose’s husband, showed up to help.

“We closed the restaurant,” Ray said. “I think everyone in the whole of Montbay County went to the wedding. The restaurant was deader than a doornail.”

With reinforcements in place, Gloria removed the apron and hung it on the hook. “I’ll go check on Margaret.”

She exited through the back porch door to round up her grandsons, who were chasing Brutus around the flowerbed, when she spied Margaret’s SUV pulling in behind Annabelle, Gloria’s car.

Gloria hurried to greet her friend and waited until she exited the vehicle. “Did you leave Don home alone?”

Margaret reached back inside, grabbed her purse and slammed the door shut. “Yeah. The old sourpuss. He told me to come without him and he needed a break because I was driving him crazy.” She rolled her eyes. “I’m driving *him* crazy?”

“So he’s home alone?” Gloria asked.

“Yeah. He mentioned his buddy, Chet, might stop by this afternoon so he should be fine,” Margaret said. “How was the wedding?”

“It was nice and simple,” Gloria said as she linked arms with her friend and they meandered around the side of the house to the back porch door. She felt bad Margaret had missed the wedding and didn’t want to rub it in.

Dot was cutting a large spiral ham when they stepped inside. “I’m glad you could make it, Margaret.”

"Me too. What can I do to help?" Margaret asked.

"Plop these babies on the rim of this bowl." Rose handed Margaret two glass bowls, a large bag of shrimp and a container of bright red liquid. "It's nice to see you out and about." Rose gave Margaret a quick hug and hurried back to the bar area.

While Margaret assembled the shrimp cocktail, Gloria darted to the front of the house to put the finishing touches on the gift table. The bride and groom, along with 100 plus guests, arrived a short time later.

The afternoon was a happy blur as Gloria buzzed back and forth between the kitchen, the newly re-wedded couple and the backyard where she attempted to keep an eye on her grandsons.

Thankfully, Paul showed up not long after and corralled the boys inside for part of the reception.

It was a wonderful afternoon of celebrating and worth every ounce of energy the friends had invested in making sure Andrea and Brian had a memorable celebration.

Margaret stayed for the festivities and even helped clean up after the majority of the guests had departed.

Gloria placed an empty punch bowl near the kitchen sink and turned to Margaret. She studied her friend's haggard face. Margaret looked tired...bone tired. Gloria placed an arm around her shoulders. "You've done more than your share to help, Margaret. Perhaps you should go home to check on Don."

Margaret nodded. "I suppose you're right. It has been so nice to escape the house and the constant bickering."

Dot overhead the conversation and shuffled across the kitchen. "He'll be up and about before you know it, Margaret. I'm sure he's just as unhappy being cooped up in the house as you are."

"True." Margaret hung her head. "I feel guilty for arguing with him. It just seems like the last couple of days, we can't even manage to say a single nice thing to each other."

Lucy wandered over to join the conversation. "We should pray."

Rose made her way over and when Ruth burst into the room, Gloria pointed at Margaret. "Margaret needs a little divine intervention."

The women circled their friend and joined hands as Gloria led them in prayer. "Dear Heavenly Father, I lift up our friend, Margaret. Lord, you know she's struggling since Don's heart attack and that they're arguing with one another. Please restore peace and quiet in the Hansen home. Thank you, in advance, for answering our prayers and thank you, most of all for our salvation. In Jesus' name. Amen."

"Amen," the girls chimed in.

Margaret wiped away a tear that had trickled down her cheek. "Thanks. I'm feeling better already." Each of the friends took turns hugging Margaret before Gloria walked her to her SUV. She waited for Margaret to climb behind the wheel before shutting the door.

Margaret rolled down the window.

"Call me if you need anything, anything at all." Gloria reached through the window and patted her shoulder. "You're not alone."

Margaret's lower lip trembled and she nodded her head. "Thanks Gloria," she whispered before she started her SUV and backed out of the driveway.

Gloria waited until her friend turned onto the road before heading back inside. Paul had taken the boys back to the farm so that Gloria and the others could clean up, and after one final sweep through Andrea's home to make sure she hadn't missed anything, she said her good-byes to Dot and Rose, who were boxing up the serving dishes and silverware.

She grabbed her purse and headed to the front hall where she found Andrea and Brian chatting with Brian's parents.

"Are you leaving?" Andrea turned, her face flushed and beaming brightly.

"I am," Gloria said. "I need to get home. It was a lovely wedding, a lovely reception."

"Thank you for everything," Andrea said. "We couldn't have done it without you."

Brian squeezed Gloria's hand. "Andrea is right. You've been a huge help and we owe you one."

"I'll take payment in the form of a grandchild." Gloria winked at Brian.

"I'll start working on it right away," Brian shot back.

"Brian." Andrea's cheeks turned a tinge of pink. "I'll call you later." She opened the front door and held it for her friend.

"Sounds good." Gloria limped across the drive to her car. Her feet were sore and her back was beginning to ache but she refused to gripe about one single ache or pain.

*Whoop. Whoop.*

Gloria spun around at the sound of the siren and hobbled to the end of Andrea's drive where an ambulance roared past. It turned onto the next street...Margaret's street.

A chill ran down Gloria's spine and she got an uncanny feeling she knew exactly where the ambulance was headed.

# Chapter 2

Andrea and Brian who had also heard the sirens, caught up with Gloria near the end of the drive. “What was that?”

“An ambulance,” Gloria said. “It turned onto the side street, heading in the same direction as Margaret’s place. I’m going to run by there just to make sure they aren’t at her house.”

“We’ll go with you,” Brian said.

The trio climbed into Gloria’s car and sped off toward Margaret’s place. When they rounded the curve, Gloria’s heart sank. Her gut instinct had been correct and an ambulance sat in her friend’s driveway.

She inched Annabelle onto the front lawn and off the street before she shifted into park. “Oh no.”

"Oh no is right," Andrea whispered as she peered out the window. "We better hang back. Maybe it's not as bad as we think."

They sat for what seemed like an eternity before a police car arrived on scene. Officer Joe Nelson hurried from his patrol car and disappeared inside the house.

Officer Nelson and the ambulance drivers were the only two on scene for at least an hour until an unmarked police car; at least Gloria suspected it was an unmarked police car, arrived. A man exited the vehicle and made his way into the house.

A knot formed in the pit of Gloria's stomach. "This doesn't look good."

Gloria reached for the door handle. "Maybe it's time to see what's going on." She flung the door open as a crime scene van pulled in behind the emergency vehicle. She released the handle and watched as a woman emerged from the vehicle carrying a large tote bag and made her way inside.

After another hour had passed, Gloria glanced at her watch. "Maybe we should leave." She stuck the car key in the ignition.

"Wait!" Andrea tapped the car window. "Look."

The ambulance drivers exited the front door, carrying a stretcher covered with a white cloth.

Gloria began to feel lightheaded and stared in disbelief at the workers, who opened the rear of the emergency vehicle and slid the stretcher inside before closing the doors. The men climbed into the front of the vehicle and slowly pulled out of the drive.

"They didn't turn the sirens on," Andrea whispered.

Several other vehicles, curiosity seekers, crept past the house but no one stopped.

"This may take a while," Brian said. "We can come back later."

"You're right. I'll take you home." Gloria started the car and slowly drove away from Margaret's home.

When they reached Andrea and now Brian's place, Gloria waited until they climbed out of the car. Andrea leaned back in before closing the door. "Keep me posted if you hear anything and I'll do the same."

After assuring her young friends she would, Gloria pulled out onto the street. She detoured past Margaret's home. The police car and crime scene van were still there so she headed home. She pulled into the drive and parked near the back porch. Before exiting the car, she sent a text message to Margaret, telling her she'd seen an ambulance out front and asking her to call because she was concerned.

Paul was inside the kitchen. "I was beginning to wonder if you got lost."

Gloria dropped her purse on the edge of the table and plopped down in the chair. The sound of a television set blared from the back of the house. "Are the boys in the living room?"

Paul nodded. "Yeah. When we got home, the boys and I checked on their tree fort and then took Mally for a walk down by the creek. We just got back."

"There's a crime scene van and a police car at Margaret's house. Earlier, there was an ambulance. Andrea, Brian and I watched them carry out a stretcher." She lowered her voice. "I'm pretty sure someone was on the stretcher, covered in a white cloth."

Paul shifted to the side. "That doesn't sound good."

"Officer Nelson showed up." Paul, a retired police officer, knew Officer Nelson. Both had worked at the Montbay County Sheriff's station. "Do you think..." Gloria's voice trailed off.

"I'll call the station to see what they know." He reached for the home phone, slipped his reading glasses on and dialed the number he knew by heart.

Gloria listened silently while Paul attempted to glean information on Margaret's situation.

"Uh-huh. I see. Well, I appreciate you letting me know. My wife is close friends with Mrs. Hansen and we're both concerned. Thank you."

Paul disconnected the line and placed the phone on the hook.

"Well? What did they say?"

Paul slowly walked to the table and slid into the chair next to his wife before reaching for Gloria's hand. "The station doesn't have all of the details yet but it looks as if Don Hansen has died."

Gloria's jaw dropped. "I..." It took several long moments for Paul's news to sink in before she burst into tears and lowered her head in her hands. Paul wrapped his arms around his wife in an effort to console her.

"Grams!" Ryan burst into the room and abruptly stopped. Tyler, who had followed his brother into the kitchen, stopped beside him.

Gloria lifted her head and attempted to stifle her sobs. "Yes boys?"

Ryan tiptoed to his grandmother's side. "What's wrong?"

Gloria closed her eyes for a moment as she struggled to compose herself. "I just got some sad news, that's all." She patted Ryan's shoulder. "I'll be okay. Why don't you and Tyler take Mally out for a few minutes and when you come back, we'll play some board games."

The boys slowly walked out the back porch door with Mally. Tyler looked back once and Gloria attempted a smile as she drew in a shaky breath.

"I-I can't believe he's gone," she whispered as she stared out the window and watched her grandsons play.

Finally, Gloria grabbed her sweater and opened the porch door. "Maybe a little fresh air will help." The barn door was open and Gloria, accompanied by Paul, wandered across the drive.

The sound of quick footsteps in the loft echoed in the cavernous barn. Gloria stood in the doorway giving her eyes a minute to adjust to the lack of light.

The smell of hay and old wood lingered in the air. It had been weeks since Gloria had stepped foot in the barn. Her eyes were drawn to the large Massey Ferguson tractor parked off to one side. The tractor had belonged to Gloria's first husband, James. Ryan and Tyler loved the old tractor and every time they visited, they begged Gloria to let them drive it.

They had taken it around the farm a few times and were getting good at maneuvering around the sheds, the barn, and even Gloria's vegetable garden. Tyler, now eleven, was tall for his age. He seemed more interested in his video games these days and less interested in the farm, the barn or the fort the boys had built the previous summer.

Ryan, on the other hand, still loved to visit the farm and to help in the garden whenever he could.

"Why don't we play catch?" Paul asked the boys as they climbed down from the hayloft. "There are a couple mitts and a ball in the garage."

"Sure." Ryan ran ahead to the garage while Tyler, Paul and Gloria followed behind. Gloria waited for Paul to pull the large wooden door across the tracks and snap the padlock shut.

The trio tossed the ball back and forth a few times while Mally chased after it. Tyler quickly grew bored and joined his grandmother on the steps. Paul and Ryan finally put away the mitts and ball and they all headed inside.

"I'll pick out the games," Tyler said as he headed to the closet and pulled out the Yahtzee and Scrabble.

Gloria popped some popcorn and poured several glasses of juice before they all settled in at the kitchen table. While they played, she kept her cell phone on the table next to her, hoping one of the other women would call but the phone never rang.

Finally, it was time for the boys to take a bath and get ready for bed.

"I'll take bath duty," Paul offered.

Gloria reached for her phone. "I'll give Dot a quick phone call." Dot would be one of the first to know what was going on since she owned the only restaurant in town, if you didn't count Kip's Bar and Grill, which mostly served munchies to the bar patrons.

Gloria headed to the porch, cell phone in hand while Paul corralled Ryan for his bath. She settled into the rocking chair and dialed Dot's cell phone. It went to voice mail and she glanced at her watch. It was close to closing time at the restaurant and more than likely Dot was busy so she tried Ruth's cell phone.

Ruth, Belhaven's postmaster, was always a wealth of information. She loved to keep up on the town's activities, the resident's activities or in other words, gossip.

"Hello?" A breathless Ruth answered on the first ring.

"Have you heard?"

"I haven't been off the phone since the ambulance pulled into Margaret's drive," Ruth groaned. "This is awful."

Ruth told Gloria that she heard from Judith Arnett, another Belhaven gossip, who heard from Sally Keane, who had once been engaged to

Officer Nelson, that Margaret found Don unresponsive in the garage.

Sally told Judith the car's engine was running and the garage door was shut. She tried shaking him and calling his name but he didn't answer so she called 911. When the EMT's and Officer Nelson arrived, they discovered Don had died.

Gloria interrupted. "Did Judith or Sally mention how Don died?" Perhaps he'd had another heart attack while trying to leave the house.

"Carbon monoxide poisoning, at least that's what they suspect."

Gloria grew quiet as she thought about Don and Margaret.

"Are you still there?" Ruth asked.

"I'm here. Just thinking," Gloria remembered how Officer Nelson arrived first and a short time later an unmarked police car pulled into Margaret's drive.

“I guess something looked suspicious to Officer Nelson so he called a detective who called the crime scene team. Has anyone heard from Margaret?” Gloria asked.

“I drove by her house a few minutes ago. The cop cars and crime scene van are gone. The porch light and her kitchen light are on but when I knocked, no one answered,” Ruth said.

“Maybe she’s down at the sheriff’s station,” Gloria said.

“Oh! Let me call you back. Sally Keane is calling.” The line went dead and Gloria set her cell phone in her lap.

Paul wandered out onto the porch. “Any news?”

Gloria repeated what Ruth had told her and Paul listened quietly until she finished. “It’s not unusual to call a detective or the crime scene investigators. Officers treat each unattended death as possibly suspect. In other words, Joe was covering his you-know-what.”

“That is why I think an unmarked police car showed up. It was probably a county detective, followed by a crime scene van,” Gloria said.

“The police need to cover all angles. Although Joe is a friend and Belhaven area resident, he still has a job to do. It’s possible Don, despondent over his health or for whatever reason, became depressed and decided to end his life. It’s also possible, considering his recent health history, that he suffered another heart attack in the car. Remember…what you heard was hearsay and might not even be accurate information. Regardless, the police are required to cover all angles.”

Gloria tapped the floor with her foot as she remembered Ruth had mentioned Margaret didn’t answer her door, which meant there was a good chance her friend was down at the sheriff’s station being questioned about Don’s death.

# Chapter 3

"I'm done!" Ryan flung the door open and sailed across the porch floor. Gloria shifted in her chair and smiled as she gazed at her grandson's sopping wet hair.

"Did you bother drying off?"

"Yeah." Ryan placed the palm of his hand on the top of his head and swiped it downward. Droplets of water splashed Gloria's leg.

"I'm hungry," Ryan said.

"I'm Grams," Gloria teased. "Okay. Let's see what I can scrounge up for you to snack on that won't get you all sugared up."

Ryan, Paul and Gloria stepped back inside and she headed to the pantry and peered inside. "You can have a granola bar, an apple or a peanut butter and jelly sandwich."

"Sandwich please." Ryan slid onto a chair and watched as she made two sandwiches, certain when Tyler emerged from the bath he would be hungry as well. She poured two glasses of milk and Tyler, right on cue, tromped into the kitchen.

"I made you a sandwich."

Tyler started to sit next to his brother before he changed his mind and walked over to Gloria, who was leaning against the kitchen counter. "I love you Grams." Her eldest grandson wrapped his arms around Gloria.

Tears burned the back of her eyes. "I love you too," she said as she held him close. "Thank you for coming to stay with us."

Ryan shoved his chair back, hopped out of his chair and raced across the kitchen floor. "I love you too Grams."

"I love you both to the moon and back." She glanced at the Tupperware container, full of raisin oatmeal cookies she'd baked the day before. She pulled them from the top of the fridge, opened the container and placed a cookie on the corner of her grandsons' plates. "I guess one little ole cookie won't hurt."

As the boys munched on their bedtime snack, they discussed what they wanted to do the following day. Jill wouldn't be picking the boys up until late afternoon. Since it was Sunday, church came first. What to do after church was up in the air and she thought she would let the boys decided.

"We can do whatever you like," Gloria said. "Within reason," she added.

Tyler took a big bite of sandwich and chewed thoughtfully. "Can we go bowling?"

"Perhaps," Gloria said.

"What about fishing?" Ryan asked.

"That's for you and Grandpa Paul to do without me." Gloria didn't hate fishing, she just didn't like it. It was, for lack of a better word, boring.

"I have an idea," Gloria said. She remembered seeing a flyer advertising a big top circus coming to the grounds of Belhaven's flea market. "Let me check something."

Gloria rummaged through the stack of junk mail in the corner of her kitchen counter where she found the bright purple flyer tucked under the pizza delivery menu. "Here it is." She slipped her reading glasses on. "There's a circus over where they have the flea market. It's today and tomorrow." She peered over the rim of her reading glasses. "Would you be interested in the circus?"

"Yes."

"No." Ryan shook his head.

"Why not?"

"Well..." Ryan kicked at the table leg. "I don't want to get trampled by an elephant."

Tyler snorted. "You're not going to get trampled by an elephant."

"Plus they stink," Ryan added.

"I can't argue with you there," Gloria said. "They have candy and other goodies at the circus." She hadn't been to the circus in decades, not since her children had been young and from what she could recall, there were some things she liked about it but others she didn't, namely the unique smells.

Paul strolled into the kitchen. "You didn't tell me we were having cookies." He reached inside the Tupperware container and pulled out a cookie. "Have you decided what you're doing tomorrow?"

"I'm leaning toward taking the boys to the circus since it's close to home." Gloria wanted to stick close to town in case Margaret needed her. Not only that, she hadn't gone bowling in years and fleeting images of throwing out her back or worse, making a fool of herself, crossed her mind. "Would you like to go with us?"

"No thanks." Paul broke off a piece of cookie and popped it into his mouth. "I'm not a fan of clowns."

"Me either." Ryan rested his chin on his hand and stared glumly at his empty plate.

"It'll be fun," Gloria said. "You've never been to the circus and you need to give it a chance."

"I guess." Shoulders slumped; Ryan picked up his plate and carried it to the dishwasher. "If I have to."

The boys placed their dirty dishes in the dishwasher and headed to the spare bedroom. Gloria followed behind. She tucked each of them into the twin beds and listened as they said their prayers.

"Dear God. Thank you for letting me spend the night with Grams. Please don't let her be sad and cry again. I pray for Mom and Dad and Mally and even Tyler. Amen. Oh and I pray the elephants don't trample me at the circus tomorrow."

Gloria, touched by both Ryan's earnest prayer that she wouldn't cry again and his fear of being trampled by an elephant, tugged at her heartstrings. She smiled as she leaned down and kissed her young grandson's forehead. "Thank you for remembering me. I'll protect you from the elephants," she promised before moving to the other bed to pray with Tyler.

Tyler's prayer included one for his "Grams" and for his parents, plus Mally.

Puddles, Gloria's cat, wandered in and leapt onto Tyler's bed. "And I pray for Puddles and that he won't wake me up in the middle of the night."

Puddles loved to sleep with the boys when they stayed, which was more like playtime for him as he attacked their toes under the blanket or chewed on their hair while they were sleeping. The cat had long since forgiven them for the time they tried to give him a bath in the toilet.

Gloria kissed Tyler's forehead and patted Puddles. "Behave yourself," Gloria warned her cat, who began to purr loudly as he cuddled up next to Tyler.

Mally, who managed to finagle her way into the room, jumped onto Ryan's bed and sprawled out next to him.

Gloria flipped the bedroom light off and turned back as the soft glow of the dining room light shone through the open doorway. "Goodnight boys. I'll see you early in the morning for Sunday School."

Paul was still in the kitchen when she wandered out. "Dot called. They just closed the restaurant and plan to have an emergency meeting of friends there."

"Did you tell them I was with Ryan and Tyler?" Gloria asked.

"I did." Paul pulled his wife to him and held her close as she placed her cheek against his chest. “I also told them I would send you down as soon as you tucked the boys in for the night.”

Gloria lifted her head and gazed into his eyes. Paul leaned down and gently kissed Gloria’s lips. For a moment, she thought about telling them she couldn’t make it and she would see them all tomorrow. “I don’t have to go,” she said when the kiss ended.

“Yes you do,” Paul said. “If not, you’ll keep us both up all night long, wondering what happened.”

“True.” Gloria took a step back. “You know me too well.” She stepped over to the door, grabbed her car keys and purse and then dropped her cell phone inside. “Hopefully I won’t be too long.”

Paul walked her to her car and waited for her to climb in before closing the door behind her. “If you don’t come back in an hour or so, I’ll send a search party out,” he teased. His expression grew serious. “If Margaret is there, please tell her how sorry I am to hear about Don.”

Paul and Gloria knew all too well what it felt like to lose a spouse. It had been a long and painful period in Gloria's life after James' unexpected death while she went through the stages of grief, the sadness, the loneliness, the heartache and finally, the loss of self. After being married for many years, it had been a difficult adjustment.

As time passed, Gloria wondered if she was meant to spend the rest of her years a widow and then without warning, God intervened and Paul entered her life. Married for less than a year now, they were still working through the honeymoon phase and learning to adjust to life together.

Right around the time they married, Paul had officially retired from the sheriff's department although he still did a little moonlighting on the side. Security detail mostly, but she secretly suspected it made him still feel useful and "in the loop."

Paul's daughter, Allie, had recently joined the sheriff's department and worked in dispatch. She had also just moved out of Paul's farmhouse and into Green Springs where she was closer to work. Gloria thought it was a smart move, although it meant that Paul's place sat empty now.

Occasionally, on weekends, they would drive to his farm and spend the night, but for the most part, they'd gotten into the habit of staying at Gloria's farm. It was closer to town and closer to Gloria's friends.

"I'll tell Margaret," Gloria promised her husband as she started the car. The drive into town was a quick trip. During the drive, Gloria prayed for her friend. She prayed for Don and for the rest of his family.

She turned Annabelle onto Main Street and parked between Ruth's van, aka spy mobile and Lucy's Jeep. Andrea's truck was parked nearby. The last vehicle she noticed was Margaret's SUV.

Gloria hurried out of the car and darted across the sidewalk. The front door to the restaurant was locked so she tapped on the large front window.

Dot, who was carrying a pot of coffee to the center table where the friends had gathered, hurried to the front to let Gloria in. "I'm glad you're here." She motioned Gloria inside and then locked the door behind her. "Margaret wanted to wait until you arrived to explain what happened."

Gloria followed Dot to the table and made her way over to Margaret. She hugged her tight. "I love you."

Margaret clung to Gloria, her head buried in her friend's shoulder. "I love you too." She finally lifted her head and gazed around the room. "I just came back from the sheriff's station. Based on the questions they asked me, they think I had something to do with Don's death."

# Chapter 4

“That’s ridiculous,” Gloria said.

“What happened?” Lucy asked.

“Start from the beginning,” Dot said.

Margaret’s hand trembled as she reached for the glass of water Rose had set in front of her. “After Brian and Andrea’s reception, I stopped by the drugstore to pick up one of Don’s prescriptions which had almost run out.”

She pursed her lips tightly together and blinked rapidly. Gloria reached over and patted her back. “It’s okay. Take your time.”

Margaret nodded. “So I picked up the prescription and also stopped at the Quik Stop to grab a carton of cookies and cream ice cream. It’s Don’s favorite and I promised to bring some home.”

Tears filled Margaret's eyes and streamed down her cheeks.

Lucy reached inside her purse, pulled out a packet of Kleenex and handed them to Margaret.

"Thanks Lucy." Margaret blew her nose before continuing. "When I got home, at first, I thought Don had gone to bed since he wasn't in the living room so I put away the purchases and stuck the containers of leftovers from the reception in the fridge so he could eat them when he woke up. I ran down to the lake to feed the duck family. When I came back inside, I decided to wake Don. I didn't want him to sleep too long and then have him wide awake all night."

Ruth, who sat on the other side of Margaret began to sniffle and then started to cry. Soon, all of the girls were crying. Ray ran over with a large box of tissues and handed them to Dot, who passed the box around the table.

Margaret wiped her eyes and continued. "When I discovered Don wasn't in the bedroom I started searching the house. When I got to the garage to see if his car was still there, that's when I found him."

She grabbed another tissue and wiped her eyes.

The women glanced at each other helplessly. There was nothing that could...or would help. "I'm sorry Margaret. What can we do?"

"I..." Margaret's voice trailed off. "Detective Givens said he would call me tomorrow. I think he felt bad he had me come in for questioning."

"He's just doing his job," Gloria said.

"I know." Margaret sipped her water and set the glass down. "I can't believe Don would...take his own life. Of course, we'd been arguing a lot lately since he was constantly underfoot and we were tripping over each other but he didn't seem depressed or despondent."

"Maybe he had a heart attack while he was getting in the car," Gloria said.

"I already thought about that but I won't know anything until the autopsy results are complete."

"I hate to see you home alone," Gloria said. "Tyler and Ryan are spending the night but I'm sure Paul won't mind if I stay with you."

"I can stay over," Lucy offered. "I'll have to bring Jasper with me."

"Ray will cut me loose for the night, too," Dot said.

"And I'm sure Johnnie would be thrilled to get me out of the house," Rose added.

"I'll go." Ruth held up her hand. "You all have spouses." She eyed Lucy. "And pets. I'm a free agent." She stood. "All I need to do is throw some clothes in an overnight bag. I'll be right back." She didn't wait for an answer as she headed out of the restaurant and climbed into her van.

Margaret watched Ruth back her van out of the parking spot and zip off down the road. "She doesn't have to do that."

"Ruth wants to help. We all want to help," Gloria said. "We're here for you Margaret."

"You can also stay at our place," Andrea offered. "We have plenty of room and Alice would love the company."

Margaret shifted her gaze to Andrea. "This is your wedding night. I didn't mean to ruin your special day."

Andrea hopped out of her chair and circled the table to hug Margaret. "You didn't ruin my day. Brian and I were already married. This was a celebration for all of us." She waved her hand around the table.

Dot replenished the empty coffee cups while Rose refilled water glasses as they waited for Ruth to return, which she did in record time. "I tried to hurry."

"I think you set some sort of record," Dot said. "Hopefully you didn't forget anything."

Margaret sipped a little more water and stood. "I think I'd like to go home now. I feel ill."

The girls accompanied Margaret and Ruth out of the restaurant and onto the sidewalk. "Are you okay to drive?" Gloria asked as she pointed at Margaret's SUV.

"Yeah." Margaret nodded. "I made it this far and it's only a couple blocks to the house. The police towed Don's car to have it examined for possible evidence." She held onto the hood of her car as she walked to the driver's side before climbing in.

Ruth hurried to her van as the others watched. "I'll call Gloria later if something comes up tonight."

"Thanks Ruth."

The group of women waited until Ruth and Margaret drove out of sight before stepping back inside the restaurant.

"We can take turns staying with Margaret," Gloria said.

"I think it makes the most sense for her to stay with me," Andrea insisted. "She shouldn't be alone."

"I agree," Lucy said. "I have plenty of room at my place, too."

"After Tyler and Ryan leave, I'll have an extra room," Gloria added.

Rose, who had been quiet for most of the meeting, spoke. "My first husband, Fred, committed suicide."

Dot shifted in her chair. "I didn't know you were married before."

"I don't share it with too many people, what with the circumstances." Rose clasped her hands and set them on the table in front of her. "We was young. Right out of high school. Fred was an angry man. We did fight but he never abused me. One night we got into a huge argument. He stomped out of the house and headed to the shed out back. I thought he was goin' out to you know, blow off some steam. Then I heard this loud popping noise so I took off runnin' to the shed and that's when I found him."

"Oh my gosh." Lucy reached over and grasped Rose's hand. "I'm sorry Rose. I had no idea."

Rose took a deep breath. "Like I said, I don't share it too much but the reason I'm tellin' you now is, if Don killed himself, you should let Margaret take the lead."

Gloria nodded. Rose spoke words of wisdom and although Gloria and her friends meant well, she could see where they might unintentionally overwhelm Margaret. "You're saying we should let her decide how much help she wants or needs."

"Yep. That would be my suggestion," Rose said.

"You're a good woman, Rose," Andrea said. "I don't care what Alice says about you."

Despite the gravity of the situation, Gloria smiled. Alice, Andrea's former housekeeper and now housemate and Rose had gotten off on the wrong foot. The women's relationship had been touch and go for some time. It was during their recent trip to Nantucket where the friends attempted to rescue Andrea the two finally started to bond.

Rose had helped Alice "dodge a bullet" literally and the women were becoming fast friends. Alice was sharing her Mexican recipes with Rose and Rose was sharing her southern style home cooking, stick-to-your-ribs comfort food with Alice.

Although the women were polar opposites in almost every way, their friendship had blossomed.

Andrea sipped her coffee and stood. "I better get home." She glanced at Gloria. "Please let me know if you hear anything."

"I will." Gloria slid out of her seat. "I better get home too. Paul is probably wondering what happened."

During the drive home, Gloria again prayed for Margaret, for Don, for Don's family. She also prayed for Rose as she thought about the guilt a young Rose had felt at her husband's death.

Gloria couldn't imagine Don killing himself. Of course, Gloria didn't live with Don and only knew what Margaret had told her and what she'd observed over the years.

She was certain the investigator would quickly clear Margaret of any wrongdoing and she could begin the mourning process without a cloud of suspicion hanging over her head.

Paul was in the living room watching television when Gloria arrived. She briefly explained what Margaret had told them and Paul agreed Don didn't seem the type to become so despondent he would take his own life.

"Remember, we only know what we hear and see for ourselves," Paul said. "You never really know someone..."

Gloria finished her husband's sentence. "Until you live with them." She headed to the bathroom to get ready for bed. Tomorrow would be a busy one, between Sunday morning church, lunch and entertaining her grandsons. She remembered her promise to Ryan and Tyler that she would take them to the circus.

Somewhere in between, she needed to reach out to Margaret, to remind her she was there if she needed anything.

Paul was already in bed by the time Gloria got there. She climbed under the covers and snuggled close to her husband. "I love you."

"I love you too." Paul tilted his head and kissed the top of his wife's head as he pulled her closer. "We're never guaranteed a tomorrow."

“That is so true,” Gloria said. “Which is why we need to appreciate every day, take the time to stop and enjoy all we have.”

“Agreed.” Paul led them in prayer. He thanked the Lord for all of their blessings, for their families, their children and grandchildren. He prayed for Margaret, for peace during this difficult time. He prayed for Andrea and Brian’s marriage, that God would guide them through the trials and tribulations of their new life together.

“Thank you most of all for Your gift of Salvation,” Paul finished.

“Amen,” they said in unison.

Gloria hugged Paul. “Thank you so much for loving me and putting up with all my crazy antics.”

Paul chuckled as he nuzzled her hair. “I wouldn’t have it any other way.”

# Chapter 5

Gloria tossed and turned all night, her concern over Margaret playing in the back of her mind, even while she was asleep.

She woke early, in a mental fog as she slipped out from under the covers, stuck her feet in her slippers and reached for her bathrobe when she remembered the boys were in the house.

Paul's soft snores assured Gloria he was still asleep so she tiptoed across the room, shooed Mally out first and then quietly closed the door behind her.

It was still dark but Gloria knew the layout of her farmhouse like the back of her hand. Mally led the way as the two headed to the kitchen. The first order of business was to let Mally outside so she opened the door and followed her onto the back porch.

The morning air was damp and Gloria shivered as she tightened the belt of her robe. Her eyes wandered to the small farm across the road. The property and farm had belonged to James' family for decades, until James' brother had run off with a woman he met on the internet and the place sat empty for years.

James eventually tired of taking care of the house and adjoining property and sold it to a local farmer who only wanted it for the land. The farmhouse sat empty for many years until the property was sold again, this time to a young family, Melody and Chris Fowler. Gloria knew Chris worked for an auto die shop in Green Springs while Melody worked as a designer at a floral shop in Rapid Creek.

Mally finished her perimeter patrol of the farm and returned to the porch. "Are you ready for breakfast?" she asked her pooch as she opened the door.

After feeding Mally and Puddles, who snuck out of the bedroom while Gloria was fixing the food dishes, she started a pot of coffee and headed back outside to grab the Sunday morning paper from the press box out front.

She unfolded the paper and glanced at the morning headline:

*"Local retired businessman and bank executive, Donald Hansen, found dead in his home."*

"Oh no," Gloria whispered as she hurried back to the house. She grabbed her cell phone, which was on the counter charging, scrolled through her contacts and pressed the text button under Ruth's name. *Don't let Margaret see the Sunday paper. Don's death is front-page news.* She pressed the "send" button and set the phone on the table.

Although the headline was huge, the article was short, probably because the newspaper didn't have much to go on yet.

*"Donald Hansen, a lifelong resident of Belhaven, Michigan and fixture in the local banking community was found dead at his home yesterday evening. Authorities are not saying what caused Mr. Hansen's death but, according to an anonymous source, officials are questioning his wife, Margaret Hansen, as well as neighbors."*

Gloria's heart pounded in her chest and she began to feel lightheaded. "Oh no. Who on earth would print such a thing?"

The article ended with the writer promising to post an update as soon as they had further information.

Gloria's cell phone beeped and she reached for her phone. Lucy had texted a message, asking if she'd seen the morning paper.

She quickly typed a reply. *Yes and I texted Ruth to hide it from Margaret.*

"What time is it?" Tyler wandered into the kitchen, rubbing his eyes.

"Time for breakfast." Gloria folded the paper and stuck it on an empty chair. She pulled out the portable griddle. "Let's make some pancakes."

While her grandsons made pancakes, Gloria began frying bacon and scrambling a dozen eggs. Paul strolled into the kitchen as she placed the last slice of cooked bacon onto a dish.

"You're just in time," Gloria said as she handed Paul a stack of plates to set the table. Paul arranged the plates, reached for the Sunday paper and paused as he read the headline. "I gather you've already seen this." He placed the paper on top of the junk pile.

"Yes. I sent Ruth a text to tell her to hide it from Margaret." She set a pitcher of orange juice in the center of the table and slid into her chair.

"Are we still going to Sunday School?" Tyler asked as he poured a glass of juice.

"Yes, of course."

After praying over their food, they passed around the platter of pancakes, eggs and bacon and Gloria reminded her grandsons they would come home after church, change, grab a quick bite to eat and head to the circus.

"I don't want to go," Ryan whined. "I dreamed an elephant trampled me last night."

"It was probably Puddles walking over the top of you," Gloria said. Puddles loved to cuddle and sleeping next to Gloria's head was his favorite nighttime activity.

Ryan placed the palm of his hand on his forehead and frowned. "Do I have to go?"

"Yes," Gloria said. "You need to at least give it a chance. If, after we get there, you don't like it, I'll have Grandpa Paul pick you up and bring you back here."

"Okay," Ryan said. "But if I get trampled, it's all your fault."

"Agreed." Gloria smiled.

Her mind drifted to Margaret as Paul and the boys discussed fishing the next time they spent the night. After they finished eating, Paul insisted she get ready for church while he and the boys cleaned up since she'd done the cooking.

It was a revolving bathroom door after Gloria finished and the boys and Paul got ready for Sunday church.

The parking lot was packed when they arrived and the only spot they were able to find was on a side street, forcing them to walk half a block to the church.

The Sunday morning church services were always crowded in the summer and fall. Attendance fell during the winter months when a number of local residents headed south to Florida or west to Arizona to escape the snow and cold.

Dot and Ray were already seated in the sanctuary when Gloria and Paul, who had dropped the boys off in the youth building, arrived. Dot slid down the bench to make room for the couple. "Did you see the Sunday paper?"

"Yes," Gloria whispered. "I texted Ruth and told her to hide it from Margaret."

"I did the same thing," Dot said.

The music began to play and they all stood for the morning worship. The service was thought provoking. Pastor Nate's message, titled, "Weathering Life's Storms," was the perfect sermon. It was as if it had been written for Margaret. The only problem was Margaret wasn't there.

Gloria jotted down the key verse:

*"For which cause we faint not; but though our outward man perish, yet the inward man is renewed day by day. For our light affliction, which is but for a moment, worketh for us a far more exceeding and eternal weight of glory; While we look not at the things which are seen, but at the things which are not seen: for the things which are seen are temporal; but the*

*things which are not seen are eternal."* 2 Corinthians 4: 16-18 (KJV)

After the service ended, Gloria and the others met in the usual spot, just outside the front entrance.

"I'll go track down Ryan and Tyler." Paul headed toward the youth building.

"Has anyone heard from Margaret or Ruth?" Dot asked.

"I haven't," Gloria said.

"Me either," Lucy added. "I can call Ruth after I get home."

"Rose and Johnnie are covering at the restaurant this morning. They have the afternoon off so Ray and I are working."

"I'm taking the boys to the circus," Gloria said. "Jill will be picking them up later this afternoon or early evening."

They agreed to let Lucy make the call and she promised she would update them after she talked to Ruth, right before she started the shut-in visits.

Back at the farm, Gloria tried again to convince Paul to join them for the trip to the circus but he told his wife he had some projects to wrap up in his woodshop and to go enjoy themselves.

Gloria, who had brought some leftovers home from Andrea and Brian's wedding reception, warmed up a dish of sweet and sour meatballs while she placed a platter of dinner rolls and sliced deli meat on the table.

The boys quickly changed and the four of them sat down to eat. After saying their blessing, Gloria handed the platter of meat to Tyler. "How was Sunday School?"

Tyler plopped a pile of meat on his plate and passed the platter to his brother. "I'm not in Sunday School Grams. I'm in the pre-teen group."

"I forgot, Tyler. You're growing up way too fast," Gloria said. "What did you do in the pre-teen group?"

Tyler told her they memorized Bible verses before working on a group-painting project while the youth pastor told them the story about the people who shouted the wall down at Jericho.

"That's a great story," Gloria said. She turned to Ryan. "What about you?"

"We learned a song," Ryan said. "It was about the Lord's army."

"Ah," Gloria nodded. "Another good one."

After lunch, the boys and Mally headed out for some fresh air while Paul helped Gloria tidy the kitchen and load the dishwasher. "I say we skip dinner tonight and head to Dot's," Paul said.

"Or maybe make it to-go and take it to Margaret," Gloria said.

"Yes, we could do that. How very thoughtful, dear." Paul hugged his wife and headed to his workshop.

Mally darted in while Paul walked out and Ryan and Tyler followed her in. "It's time to get going. We don't want to be late." Gloria glanced at the clock above the kitchen sink.

"I've got a stomach ache," Ryan moaned. "Maybe I should just stay here."

"No. You're going to go." Gloria shook her head firmly. "You promised to give the circus a chance." During the drive to the flea market/circus grounds, Tyler chattered excitedly while Ryan sat glumly in the passenger seat. He still wasn't keen on visiting the circus but when they arrived and pulled into an empty parking spot, he spotted a row of carnival games, which perked him up.

Happy that her grandson was finally coming around, she gave each of them some money to play a few of the games, including popping balloons with darts and toss the rings. They finished spending their money and then wandered to the animal pens located behind the big top.

Thankfully, there were no elephants in sight and after visiting the animals; they headed inside the big top to find seats. Gloria spotted concession stands off to one side and let each of the boys pick a treat to eat before wandering to the bleachers.

Gloria waved at several locals before they settled onto a bench seat near the center, but not too close to the bottom at Ryan's insistence.

The show was more entertaining than Gloria thought it would be and her favorite part was the trapeze artists. Tyler seemed to like everything while Ryan fidgeted in his seat, warily keeping an eye out for elephants on a rampage.

When the motorcycle stunt drivers roared onto the stage, Ryan sat up in his seat and watched with rapt attention as the ear-splitting motorcycles raced up makeshift ramps and became airborne in a series of death-defying stunts. After they finished their part of the show and sped off the stage, Ryan tugged on Gloria's arm. "I want to be a motorcycle stunt driver someday."

Gloria grinned, thrilled he was finally excited about some part of the show. "Be sure to tell that to your mother when you see her." She could just envision Jill's reaction when she found out her youngest child wanted to become the next Evil Knievel.

"I'm gonna ask for a dirt bike for Christmas," he added.

Next was the jugglers, followed by the clowns and Ryan shrank back in the seat as the clowns and jugglers circled the arena. "I hope they don't come up here," Ryan whispered.

Tyler lifted his Slurpee and took a big gulp. "Me either. I hate clowns."

"What is it about clowns you two don't like?" Gloria asked. When she was young, clowns were fun, entertaining. These days, kids feared clowns. In fact, she'd heard on the news there was a man dressed as a clown who stalked kids on their way home from school.

"They stab people," Tyler said. "They're not real clowns," he added matter-of-factly, "but people who dress like clowns and attack people, mostly kids."

The show finally ended and the trio waited for the crowds to thin before making their way down the bleacher stairs and exiting the tent.

"Don't forget to toss your empty drink cups and boxes." Gloria pointed to a trashcan a short distance from the big top entrance.

Tyler and Ryan zigzagged past a group of young people as they made their way to the trashcan. Tyler dropped his trash inside while Ryan tipped his head back and dropped the last

M&M in his mouth before he tossed the empty box inside.

"Uh-oh." Gloria watched as a tall clown with curly red hair sauntered across the gravel path. He was carrying something in his hand and she couldn't tell what it was.

"Ryan!" Gloria hollered, hoping to get her grandson's attention.

It was too late. Ryan spun around and came face-to-face with the clown. He let out an ear-piercing scream. "Agh!"

The clown made a sudden movement, as if to take a step back but Ryan was too fast. He grabbed the clown's bright orange hair and yanked on it, pulling his wig off.

The clown lunged for his wig. Ryan, his eyes wide with terror, threw the wig at the clown and kicked him squarely between the legs.

# Chapter 6

The clown fell to the ground and began groaning.

Gloria ran over and attempted to assist the clown, who was lying in a fetal position writhing in pain.

"He tried to attack me," Ryan gasped.

Gloria grabbed Ryan's arm and tugged him back. "Stay over here." She knelt next to the injured clown. "I'm so sorry. My grandson got scared. He doesn't like clowns."

"It's okay," the clown whispered. "He's the second kid today who attacked me. I think I'm gonna apply for the sword swallower's job. It's not as dangerous."

"You're probably right." Gloria helped the man to his feet and plucked the wig from the ground.

She handed it to him and apologized again. "I'm so sorry."

"It's okay." The clown limped away and Gloria joined her grandsons who stood off to one side.

"I didn't mean to kick him," Ryan said as they slowly walked to the car. "I just freaked out."

Gloria put an arm around her grandson's shoulders. "I'm partly to blame. You told me you didn't want to come to the circus. At least you weren't attacked by an elephant."

Ryan shuddered. "Yeah."

"It wasn't a real clown," Tyler said. "He was just dressed up as a clown."

They climbed into the car and after the boys buckled their seatbelts, Gloria pulled out of the parking lot and onto the street. When she reached Main Street, she turned left, deciding to drive by Margaret's place.

Ruth's van wasn't there. Lucy's jeep was, so she pulled in behind it.

"Where are we?" Ryan reached for the door handle.

"We're at my friend, Margaret's house. You remember Margaret."

"I think so. I gotta use the bathroom."

"We'll head back to the farm." Gloria shifted the car in reverse.

"I have to go now," Ryan insisted as he squirmed back and forth. "I can't wait."

"Very well then." She shut the car off and they climbed out. Ryan hopped to the sidewalk while Tyler ran ahead to ring the doorbell.

Moments later, Lucy appeared. She waved them into the breezeway. "I called the house and Paul told me you took the boys to the circus."

"It was fun," Gloria said.

"Except for the end when Ryan attacked a fake clown," Tyler said.

"I have to go to the bathroom." Ryan began to hop on one foot, his signal he really needed to use the restroom.

"Margaret is taking a nap." Lucy held a finger to her lips. "We'll have to be quiet."

Gloria brought up the rear and followed the others into the mudroom. "The half bath is over here." She led her grandson to the bathroom and flipped the light on. "We'll be in the kitchen."

"Coffee?" Lucy stood in front of the kitchen counter. "I made a small pot for myself while I waited for Margaret to wake up."

"How is she doing?" Gloria asked.

"I haven't talked to her yet. When I called after church, Ruth told me she had some errands to run so I offered to come by. By the time I got here, Margaret was already taking a nap."

"Can I go down to the lake?" Tyler reached for the slider handle that led to the rear deck and to Margaret's backyard.

"Yes, but stay out of the water." Fall was right around the corner. Although the days were still pleasant, the evenings were chilly and the water too cold for swimming.

"I wanna go!" Ryan burst into the kitchen.

"Shh..." Gloria whispered. "You can both go."

The boys disappeared outside and Gloria turned her attention to Lucy. "Did Ruth happen to say how Margaret was doing?"

"Margaret is having a nightmare." Margaret shuffled into the kitchen. "Hello Gloria. Welcome to my nightmare."

Gloria's heart sank as she gazed at her friend. Margaret prided herself on her meticulous grooming. She wore designer duds and her hair was always styled in the latest fashion...but not today. Her short, perky spikes were matted to her head and she was wearing a tattered housecoat.

Gloria glanced at her bare feet. Margaret never went barefoot. “I wish it was only a bad dream.” She pulled out a chair. “Why don’t you sit down?”

Margaret eased into the chair and stared blankly at Gloria. “Ruth must have given me some good stuff before I went to bed. I was out like a light.”

The boys darted past the slider.

“Someone is on my deck.”

“It’s Ryan and Tyler. I took them to the circus and thought I would stop by here to check on you on my way home.”

“What day is it?” Margaret asked.

“Sunday,” Lucy said. “It’s Sunday.”

“Sunday...” Margaret pondered the words. “Don died yesterday.”

“Yes,” Gloria said.

Margaret ran a hand through her hair. "I need to think about the funeral, don't I?"

Gloria sat next to Margaret. "We'll help you, Margaret. All of us, if you want."

"I talked to Chad last night after I got home. He's flying in and should be here sometime today." Chad was Don and Margaret's only child, a son who lived in Albuquerque. He'd gone off to college in California and after getting his CPA license, moved to Albuquerque.

"I'm glad he's on his way," Gloria said.

The slider flew open and Tyler ran inside. "Grams! Come quick!"

Gloria's heart skipped a beat. *Come quick* were two words she never liked to hear together, not from one of her grandsons. It meant something had happened and more than likely, it wasn't good.

Gloria jogged across the kitchen and followed Tyler onto the deck. He was halfway down the sloped back lawn, running at breakneck speed. She could see Ryan near the shoreline. He was kneeling on the ground next to the wooden dock that led out to Lake Terrace.

She came to an abrupt halt behind her grandsons. Ryan hovered over a nest of fuzzy yellow birds. "Look at the baby ducks."

Lucy and Margaret quickly caught up with them. "It's a little late in the year for baby ducks," Lucy said.

"Don't touch them," Gloria said. "We need to leave the ducks here so the momma duck can find them. I bet that's the momma now."

A mottled brown bird with blue-purple tipped feathers swam toward them and waddled onto shore.

The group took stepped back as the duck made her way to the chirping birds. The bird circled the chicks several times before leading them into the water and they paddled off.

Margaret attempted a small smile. "I wondered what happened to my ducks. I kept bringing out food for them but thought they had moved on."

"They've been busy," Lucy joked. "I thought most ducks were born in the spring."

"Me too," Gloria said. "I guess they didn't get the memo."

"The cycle of life," Margaret said as they retraced their steps. "Life, death, marriage. I guess we've seen it all in the last day."

Gloria linked arms with her friend. "And God shall wipe away all tears from their eyes; and there shall be no more death, neither sorrow, nor crying, neither shall there be any more pain: for the former things are passed away."

"Revelation 21, Verse 4," Lucy said. "I memorized the verse when Gary died."

The boys headed to the front yard to inspect Margaret's trees for "fort worthiness" and the women made their way back inside.

Lucy closed the door behind them. "I made some coffee. You'll need to warm it in the microwave."

"Thanks." Margaret wandered to the cupboard, grabbed a clean cup, filled it with coffee and stuck it in the microwave. "Detective Givens told me he would call today. He said the autopsy results should be in."

The microwave beeped and Margaret pulled the cup out. "I just can't believe Don would want to end his life. It doesn't add up. Just the other day he told me when he was thinking of starting a part-time financial consulting business to give him something to do during the long winter months. It was either that or become snowbirds and spend our winter months in Florida where he could golf and play tennis."

Gloria sat in the seat across from Margaret and drummed her fingers on the tabletop. “You knew Don better than any of us but he didn’t seem depressed, not even after the heart attack.”

“He seemed fine when I left to head over to Andrea and Brian’s reception. He even reminded me to bring the ice cream home.” Margaret’s lower lip quivered. “I just don’t understand.”

The doorbell chimed. “That must be Ryan and Tyler.” Gloria sprang from her chair and hurried to the front door, wondering why the boys didn’t just come back in through the kitchen door.

She swung the door open. On the other side was a man Gloria didn’t recognize.

“Can I help you?”

“Yes. I’m Detective Givens. Is Mrs. Hansen home?”

# Chapter 7

"I'll be right back." Gloria slammed the door in the detective's face and hurried to the kitchen. "Margaret, Detective Givens is here to see you."

"Where is he?" Lucy shifted in her chair.

"I left him on the front porch," Gloria said.

Margaret waved her hand. "Might as well let him in."

Gloria darted to the front door and flung it open. "I wanted to check to make sure she was ready for company. Follow me." She led him into the kitchen.

Lucy popped out of her chair. "We should get going."

Margaret lifted her hand and eyed the detective warily. "No. Please stay."

"This shouldn't take long," the detective said. "We got the autopsy results back. We found a sedative in your husband's bloodstream, more than someone would take if they planned to get behind the wheel of a car and drive somewhere."

The detective shifted his feet. "In fact, it's possible he may not have even been able to walk to the vehicle on his own."

"You think someone put him in the car?" Gloria asked.

The detective ignored Gloria's question. "I'll need an exact timeline of your whereabouts yesterday, Mrs. Hansen. Where you went, who you talked to, what you did."

"She needs an alibi," Lucy whispered. "You think Margaret drugged her husband, dragged him to his car, turned it on and killed him with carbon monoxide poisoning?"

"We're not ruling anyone or anything out," the detective said. "As I said a moment ago, we aren't sure Mr. Hansen would have been able to walk to the garage, climb inside his vehicle and start it. He was sedated."

The detective asked several questions regarding Don's acquaintances and his recent activities.

"He's been staying close to home since his heart attack. Maybe he got confused and took too much of one of his prescriptions," Margaret said.

"I would like to look at his cell phone. We need to check his phone records and recent calls."

"I'll go get it." Margaret pushed her chair back and walked out of the room. She returned a short time later, empty-handed. "I can't find it."

"Try calling it," Lucy suggested.

"That's a good idea." Margaret made her way over to the kitchen counter, picked up her cell phone and turned it over. She pressed several buttons. "It's ringing."

“It went to voice mail,” she reported before hitting the end button and setting the phone down. “Maybe the battery died. Don never was good at remembering to charge his phone.”

“Maybe he left it in his car,” Gloria said.

“I’ll have someone check.” The detective jotted some notes on the pad of paper he was holding. He asked Margaret several more pointed questions, about her and Don’s relationship and if they were having marital or financial difficulties.

“Our finances are fine. We had been driving each other crazy since his recent heart attack and he was underfoot but nothing serious,” Margaret said.

The detective flipped the pad of paper shut and shoved it in his pocket. “Please look for the cell phone and let me know when you find it.” He asked for the name of their cell phone carrier and Gloria guessed he planned to request a copy of the phone records from them.

Margaret gave him the information and assured him she would search for the phone before Gloria escorted the detective out. She watched Detective Givens climb into his car and drive off before she shifted her gaze as she searched for her grandsons. They were nowhere in sight.

"I need to track down the boys," Gloria hollered into the kitchen before stepping outside.

She circled the house and found them darting back and forth in the side yard. "What are you doing?"

Tyler looked up. "Someone dumped this confetti paper all over the yard." He held up a wad of shredded paper in one hand and a plastic grocery store bag with a large tear in it in the other. "The bag ripped."

"We're picking it up cuz it's blowing all over." Ryan pointed toward the nearby pine tree and the bits of shredded paper surrounding the base.

“That’s very nice of you,” Gloria said. “I’ll see if Margaret has another bag you can use to put them in.” She hurried back inside the house where Lucy and Margaret were still sitting at the kitchen table. “The boys are picking up some shredded paper. It looks like it blew out of your recycle bin.”

Margaret frowned. “I didn’t shred anything.” She hurried to her pantry, grabbed a couple empty plastic bags and headed out the back door where the boys were still scrambling around, picking up the pieces.

She handed each of them an empty bag. “Thank you Ryan and Tyler. Don must have shredded something the other day and stuck the bag in the recycle bin.”

Lucy and Gloria trailed behind and stood next to Margaret.

“Don always left a shred pile for me to take care of,” Margaret said. “I’m surprised he knew how to use the shredder.”

After they finished picking up the bits of paper, Gloria's grandsons tied the bags shut and handed them to Margaret, who tucked them under a stack of bundled newspapers so they wouldn't blow away again.

Gloria glanced at her watch. "We better get going. I'm sure Paul is beginning to wonder if we ran away with the circus." The boys raced each other to the car and climbed in the backseat.

Gloria hugged her friend. "Let me know if you need anything Margaret."

Margaret embraced Gloria and then took a step back. "I will. I'll feel much better once Chad gets here."

"I'll stay a little longer and then head out to start the visits to the shut-ins," Lucy said.

"It's been so hectic, I almost forgot. I'll handle next Sunday's visits." Gloria promised as she reached for the car door handle. "I'll call you in the morning," she told Margaret before shutting the door and backing out of the drive.

By the time they reached the farm, the boys were hungry again so she threw a frozen pizza in the oven and made her way to the workshop to check on Paul. He had recently begun refurbishing her dining room hutch. The hutch was an heirloom piece passed on to her by her mother. The top and front had become battered and scuffed after decades of use.

Paul was doing a wonderful job restoring the hutch and it was starting to look like new. “I’m back,” she hollered through the open door.

Paul dropped the piece of sandpaper in his hand on top of the hutch. “I was beginning to think I needed to call out a search party.”

Gloria wandered over to the workbench and ran a light hand across the top of the hutch’s smooth surface. “I stopped by Margaret’s house after the circus to check on her.”

“How is she doing?”

“Okay. The investigator showed up while I was there. Judging by the conversation and questions, Detective Givens doesn't think Don's death was an accident and Margaret isn't off the hook. Her son, Chad, will be here later today."

Paul nodded. "How was the circus? I take it you kept Ryan safe from being attacked by the elephants."

Gloria rolled her eyes. "Yes, but the clown is another story." She told her husband how the clown had scared Ryan and how he had yanked off his wig and kicked him between the legs.

"Ouch." Paul grimaced. "There's never a dull moment when those two are around."

"You've got that right. Speaking of which, I threw a frozen pizza in the oven. Despite the fact I bought them goodies at the circus, they're both starving."

Paul followed his wife out of the workshop. He shut off the light and closed the door behind them. "I'm not hungry right now, but I thought since you've been busy this weekend with the boys, I might be able to entice you into letting me take you out for a romantic dinner this evening at Garfield's instead of Dot's."

Garfield's was a bed and breakfast/restaurant located on the shores of Lake Harmony. It was in nearby Rapid Creek. Paul had taken Gloria there for dinner a few months back. It was a lovely Victorian home with an elegant period interior that reminded Gloria of days gone by.

"It sounds lovely. Hopefully Jill picks them up before it gets too late."

"If not, we can do it later in the week," he promised.

The boys, who had been playing upstairs, bounded down the stairs just as Gloria pulled the pizza from the oven. Between the two of them, they ate the entire pizza and were heading outdoors when Lucy pulled in the drive.

"I wonder what Lucy's doing here," Gloria mumbled under her breath as she stepped onto the porch.

The skies had turned overcast and a stiff breeze whipped Gloria's bangs into her eyes. She smoothed them off to the side and headed down the steps. Her first thought was something had happened to Margaret.

Her second thought was perhaps something had happened to one of the shut-ins Lucy planned to visit. Eleanor Whittaker, an elderly woman who lived in a rambling house overlooking Lake Terrace, was one of the area residents the Garden Girls now visited weekly.

Eleanor had had a string of mishaps and taken several spills. The previous week, she'd almost set her house on fire. Gloria was concerned for her friend and worried that living alone was becoming dangerous.

Gloria's fears were confirmed when Eleanor admitted she forgot she'd lit a small candle on the kitchen counter when she opened her kitchen window. A roll of paper towels had somehow managed to unravel and the tip caught fire since the candle was directly beneath the roll.

Thankfully, Eleanor had wandered back into the kitchen to make a cup of tea when she discovered the burning paper towels and had managed to extinguish the fire.

Gloria was on the fence about contacting Eleanor's family to voice her concerns since she didn't want to overstep her boundaries and be blamed if Eleanor was forced to move from the only home she'd ever known, but she also didn't want to see anything happen to the sweet lady.

She finally decided if there was one more incident, she would have no choice but to contact Eleanor's children.

"Oh, I'm so glad you're here. I thought maybe you would be running the boys home," Lucy said.

"No. I'm waiting for Jill to pick them up. She usually calls me when she's on the way but I haven't heard from her yet. Is everything okay? Is Eleanor okay?"

“Eleanor is fine,” Lucy said. “In fact, she asked where you were. I told her Ryan and Tyler were visiting so you couldn’t make it.”

“I’ll stop by her place this week,” Gloria said. “Maybe I can bring her down to Dot’s for coffee and donuts. I’m sure she would like to get out of the house.”

“I agree.” Lucy nodded. “I wanted to tell you before I left Margaret’s house, I ran outside to gather her mail because she didn’t want to go out. After I brought the mail in the house, I stayed for a few more minutes and Margaret began sorting through it.”

“That was thoughtful of you Lucy,” Gloria said.

“Thanks. I started to leave when Margaret got this funny look on her face. I asked her if everything was okay and she handed one of the pieces of mail she’d opened to me.”

“What was it?”

“It was a notice from Margaret’s bank, telling her that her checking account was overdrawn.”

# Chapter 8

"Overdrawn?" Gloria stared at Lucy blankly. "How is that possible?" Don, a former bank vice president, was a stickler for numbers, for making sure he and his wife were in pristine financial shape. He'd spent his entire career making sure that once he retired, Margaret and he would be set for the rest of their lives.

Margaret had once confided in Gloria they had numerous retirement accounts, IRA's, Roth IRA's, CDs, a 401k as well as regular savings accounts. "Maybe Don was getting ready to cash in one of the retirement accounts and forgot to take care of it."

"I don't know." Lucy shook her head. "All I know is Margaret was rattled. She kept saying she couldn't believe it and as soon as I left, she was going to log onto the internet and check the accounts to see what was going on."

"You don't think..." Gloria's voice trailed off. *What if Don had wiped out their life savings? What if there wasn't any money?* It would give someone reason to contemplate taking their own life. She hoped it wasn't the case. "I'm sure she'll get it straightened out."

"I hope so. She was shook up." Lucy left after telling Gloria she needed to head home to let Jasper out.

While Gloria walked back to the house, she mulled over Margaret's situation. She hoped Don hadn't squandered all of their retirement money. He would have to do a lot of squandering.

She thought about the money Margaret and she, along with her sister, Liz, had gotten after selling the valuable coins they'd found in the mountains at "Aunt Ethel's" place.

Gloria tidied the kitchen and bathroom, keeping one eye on the clock. With every minute that passed, she grew more concerned about her daughter and finally decided to give Jill a jingle to make sure everything was all right.

She picked up her cell phone only to realize she'd turned the volume down. There was a missed call from her daughter, telling her Greg and she had run into some car problems on their drive home and had just gotten back. She told her mother she was on the way.

Gloria erased the message and turned the volume up before she glanced at the clock. It was too late to dine at Garfield's. It was already after six.

Paul stepped into the kitchen. "Any news from Jill?"

"She's on her way. I don't have the details but she said they had car problems on the drive home. I'm afraid it will be too late to go out to dinner by the time she leaves."

Paul pulled his wife into his arms. "We'll do it later this week or next weekend," he promised. "Why don't we run down to Dot's instead? You can kill two birds with one stone...you won't have to cook dinner and you can maybe find out if anyone has heard anything else on Margaret's situation."

"Oh. Lucy stopped by. You'll never guess what happened." Gloria told Paul about the notice from the bank that Margaret's checking account was overdrawn.

Paul released his grip. "Poor Margaret." He shook his head. "Why don't I take the boys down to the creek to see if it's come up yet? By the time we get back, Jill will be here."

Paul leaned into the dining room. "Hey boys! Do you want to go back to the creek to check on the water level?"

Muffled feet stampeded across the floor and a breathless Ryan and Tyler raced into the kitchen. "Sure!"

They slid their feet into their shoes and slipped their windbreakers on.

"Don't get wet or muddy," Gloria warned them before they darted out the door.

"I'll try my best to keep them clean," Paul promised before he kissed his wife and followed them out.

She watched through the window as the trio strode across the yard and disappeared from sight.

Her eyes were drawn to her cell phone and she picked it up, dialing Margaret's home phone before she could change her mind.

Margaret answered on the first ring.

"Hi Margaret. It's me, Gloria. Has Chad arrived yet?"

"His plane landed already and he is on his way to pick up his rental car. He'll be here within the hour."

“I’m glad to hear he’s on his way,” Gloria said. “How are you doing?” She didn’t dare mention Lucy had stopped by to tell her about the overdrawn bank account. She didn’t want her friend to think they were gossiping about her.

“Not good.” Margaret told her what Lucy had already said, how the bank had sent a notice in the mail about her overdrawn checking account.

“Oh my goodness. Did you get it straightened out?”

“No,” Margaret said. “I tried to pull up our accounts on line and every single password has been changed. The only one I could get into was my own, the one I opened last year. It’s where I put the money we got from the coins.”

Gloria’s scalp tingled. Perhaps Don had taken all the money...and done what? “Maybe Don recently changed the account numbers. Did you try checking the box you forgot your password so you could reset them?”

"I did. I tried to log into Don's email account and that password has been changed, too."

Something was wrong…terribly wrong. Gloria had a sinking feeling whatever had happened to Don was somehow tied to their finances. Margaret voiced Gloria's thoughts.

"What if Don cleaned out our accounts, somehow lost all of our retirement and savings and instead of confess what had happened, he became despondent and killed himself?"

Gloria's head spun. It was a thought. Money made people do crazy things. "But what would he have done with all of the money? It doesn't make sense. He was so meticulous about making sure you two had enough to comfortably live out the rest of your years."

"I know, but I'm beginning to wonder," Margaret said. "Remember how the boys found those shredded bits of paper in the recycle bin? Don never shredded anything. He always left if for me to take care of. Maybe he was trying to hide something."

"So now what?"

"I'll have to wait until tomorrow to sort this out. The only problem is our accounts were all over the place, not just our bank. We had investment accounts through a variety of sources. It's going to take some time to untangle."

"Do you need money to get by?" Gloria asked. "We can help out."

"I appreciate the offer, Gloria. I haven't touched the money we got from the coins. It will tide me over for a very long time. I only have my living expenses. The house, the SUV, everything is owned free and clear."

Gloria opened her mouth to reply and quickly closed it. *What if Don had mortgaged the house? Margaret would have had to co-sign if the house was in both their names.*

"I hate to be nosy, but is the house in your name, too?" Gloria asked.

"Yes, thankfully. If Don were up to funny business, he wouldn't have been able to take a loan out on the place without my signature. Oh, Chad just pulled in the drive. I'll call you back."

"Okay, Margaret. Keep me posted." Gloria told her friend good-bye and disconnected the line. She set the phone down and closed her eyes to pray. She prayed there was some misunderstanding, that Don hadn't squandered all of their retirement money and for some reason, he had changed the accounts around and forgot to tell his wife.

Gloria headed to the porch and settled into one of the rocking chairs to wait for her daughter and for Paul and her grandsons to return. The sun had set and there was a pink-purple tinge to the skyline. It was a beautiful late summer evening.

Soon, it would be fall and time for festivals, pumpkin patches, hayrides and apple cider. It was one of Gloria's favorite times of the year. Winter was her least favorite and it seemed the older she got the less she liked it.

Paul and she had tossed around the idea of becoming part-time snowbirds. Liz, Gloria's sister, who lived in Florida, had been bugging her to come down and visit.

Gloria nudged the floor with her foot and rocked back as she stared at the barn. Maybe it was time. There was nothing to stop them from going. The thought of sunny winter days and balmy winter nights was tempting.

She remembered the honeymoon Paul and she had taken to Florida. They'd had a lovely time, although it had been somewhat stressful and Gloria had ended up breaking her leg.

Paul loved to fish. If they spent a few months near the ocean, he could fish to his heart's content. Gloria could take in some local flea markets. Maybe they could even try a new hobby like golf. Florida was full of golf courses.

It sounded more appealing than staying cooped up inside the house for months on end.

The sound of tires on her gravel drive pulled Gloria from her musings and she smiled as she saw Jill, who was driving her husband's pick-up truck, pull into the drive.

Gloria slid out of the rocker and made her way down the steps. She met Jill in the drive and hugged her daughter. "I'm sorry to hear of your car problems. Did you get them fixed?"

"Yes," Jill groaned. "We got a flat on the highway. We must've picked up a nail or screw somewhere along the way. Greg put the spare, the donut tire on the front and we limped home. He's going to take it to the auto place first thing in the morning to get a new tire and check the others to make sure we didn't pick up anything else along the way."

Jill followed her mother to the porch. "How are the boys? Did they behave themselves? How was Andrea's wedding?"

Gloria told her the wedding was lovely, the boys were fine and then she told her about the clown incident.

"Oh my gosh!" Jill clamped a hand over her mouth to hide her grin. "I can't believe you convinced Ryan to go to the circus in the first place. You can blame Tyler for his paranoia. He let his brother watch one of those scary clown/nightmare movies and now Ryan is convinced a clown is going to attack him."

"Or an elephant," Gloria added.

"Yes, or an elephant."

"Mom!" Ryan, Tyler and Paul emerged from the field and Ryan raced across the yard and drive to where the women stood chatting. "Grandpa Paul said next time we come over he's going to take us fishing. We get to catch them and clean them and everything!"

Jill hugged her young son. "That sounds like lots of fun." She ruffled Tyler's hair when he got close. "I heard your brother had a run in with a clown."

Tyler grunted. "Yeah. He gave him a swift kick between the legs and ripped his wig off."

"I thought he was going to attack me," Ryan said.

"Go grab your stuff. Your dad is home fixing dinner," Jill said.

The boys raced inside the house.

While they were gone, Gloria briefly told Jill about Don's death. The boys returned before Gloria could go into detail.

Ryan tugged on Gloria's hand. "Thanks for letting us stay Grams. Maybe next time we can sleep in the tree fort."

"Of course." Gloria kissed her grandsons and she and Paul waited until they were in the truck and on the road before heading back inside.

“Those two are go, go go.” Paul shook his head. “I wish I could bottle a quarter of their energy.”

“Me too.”

“Are you ready to head down to Dot’s? I’m afraid if I hit the recliner I might not want to get back up,” Paul confessed.

“Me either,” Gloria agreed. On the short ride into town, Gloria told Paul about her conversation with Margaret, how their account passwords had been changed and how Don had changed his email password so Margaret couldn’t access his account.

She also told him about the shredded paper the boys had found scattered in Margaret’s yard and Margaret’s comment Don never shredded anything.

“You think whatever happened to Don had something to do with their finances.” Paul tightened his grip on the steering wheel. “Love and money. Two of the top reasons crimes are committed.”

“And the love of money,” Gloria added.

# Chapter 9

Business was booming at Dot's and Paul had to drive around the block just to find an empty parking spot. They ended up parking in front of Nails and Knobs, Brian's hardware store, and walked to the other end of Main Street.

The place was packed but Paul and Gloria found a corner table for two, near the server station. Bea McQueen, a local hairdresser, and Ruth were seated two tables over. Gloria gave them a quick wave before pulling out her chair and sitting.

She also spotted Al Dickerson, Liz's old flame, and Glen Shenk, one of the retired locals who ate, breathed and slept fishing. Paul had gone fishing with Glen a couple times and told his wife that Glen was the fish whisperer.

Rose hurried over, menus in hand. "Good gracious sakes, we're busy for a Sunday night." She placed two menus on the table.

"Margaret," Gloria said.

"Margaret? She's here?" Rose's eyes scanned the dining room.

"No. Margaret is the reason people are here. Whenever something happens in Belhaven it brings out the locals," Gloria said.

"Ah." Rose lifted a brow. "I swear I may never get used to livin' in a small town." She clasped her hands. "What can I getcha?"

"I don't need to look at the menu since I know it by heart," Gloria said. "I'll take a cheeseburger with everything and an order of French fries."

"Would you like to sample something new?" Rose asked. "We're testing my black-eyed peas and ham hock. It comes with my made-from-scratch cornbread. Both are secret family recipes."

"Okay. Let me try that instead," Gloria said. "I'm sure with your southern cooking skills, it's delicious."

"It'll make you wanna swaller yer tongue."

Gloria's eyes widened. "Swallow my tongue?"

Rose waved a hand. "It's a southern sayin'. Just means it's good eatin."

Paul shut his menu. "I'll have the same."

"That's my man." Rose winked at Paul and reached for the menus. "I brewed a fresh pot of coffee. I'll be back with a couple cups."

"You know us too well," Gloria said. She watched Rose head to the back and turned her attention to the other diners. "It's going to be strange not passing Don on the roads or seeing him and Margaret in here for dinner."

She shifted in her seat and focused her gaze on her husband. "You know as much as I do. What do you think happened to Don?"

Rose returned with two glasses of ice water and two coffees and Paul waited until she left to answer his wife's question. "What we know is Don recently argued with someone on the golf course which may have triggered his heart attack."

"The argument caused a lot of stress," Gloria said. "Not to mention losing all his and Margaret's life savings, if that's the case."

"Don also told Margaret he was thinking about taking on some part-time work. He told her it was to keep him busy but maybe they were in deep financial straits."

Gloria peeled the paper off her straw and shoved it in her glass of water before continuing. "Shredded papers in the recycle bin, a notice from the bank stating their account was overdrawn and the password on their accounts, not to mention Don's email account was changed."

"He was keeping something from Margaret. I can feel it in my bones." Gloria reached for her cup of coffee.

"I'm never one to jump to conclusions, but I have to admit all the signs are pointing in that direction," Paul said. "What about the person or persons Don argued with at the country club? What's the story?"

Holly, Dot and Rose's part-time employee, arrived with their food. She set the bowls of black-eyed peas and ham on the table. Under the peas was a thick bed of white rice. She slid a bowl of fresh cornbread muffins off to the side. "You are going to love this," Holly said. "I was hesitant at first to try it but oh boy, this is some good stuff."

Gloria reached for her fork but after studying the dish, decided on a soupspoon instead. She dipped the spoon in the bowl and scooped it into her mouth. The salty ham mixed with the earthy flavor of the black-eyed peas was an interesting combination.

After her first bite, she wasn't sure what she thought. The second bite was better and by the third spoonful, Gloria was hooked. She reached for a warm muffin. "What do you think of the food?"

"It's an acquired taste," Paul said. "But good. What do you think of the texture?"

"It's...unique, but in a good way."

Rose stopped by to get their opinion and Gloria gave her a thumbs up. "It's a keeper."

Rose beamed. "I admit now. It takes a couple bites to grab ya, but when it does...hang on." She was still smiling as she made her way to a nearby table to check on the diners.

Paul reached for a cornbread muffin. "You don't have any details about the person Don argued with the day of his heart attack?"

"No." Gloria shook her head. "I guess at the time I didn't give it much thought but now it might be a clue. I'm sure Margaret knows who it was."

Margaret and Don were members of the local country club. They had been members for decades and knew most, if not all, of the other members. She made a mental note to ask her friend when she talked to her.

They finished their meal and Ruth and Bea stopped by to say hello. They didn't discuss Margaret and Gloria was relieved. Bea was a colossal busybody. She had her nose stuck in everyone's business and Gloria suspected she'd invited Ruth to dinner to pump her for information about Margaret.

"I'll call you later." Ruth gave Gloria a meaningful stare before she followed Bea out of the restaurant.

Dot stopped by looking frazzled and stressed.

"You look like you could use a break," Gloria said.

Dot tucked a stray strand of hair behind her ear. "I probably could. I'm feeling slightly nauseous."

"That settles it." Gloria pushed her chair back. "I'll be right back."

"Take your time." Paul reached for another muffin.

Gloria led Dot through the kitchen and out the rear door to the employee picnic table. "Have a seat. I'll get you a glass of water."

Gloria hurried back inside and to the server area where she grabbed a clean glass and filled it with ice and water before rejoining Dot.

"Thanks." Dot took the glass of water and sipped. "I feel better already."

"The point of co-owning the restaurant was so you and Ray could take it easy and semi-retire."

"I know." Dot held up a hand. "We just got crushed tonight. I think it's because of not only Brian and Andrea's wedding but also Don's death."

"I agree," Gloria said. She told Dot about her conversation with Margaret, how Don had changed the passwords to their accounts.

Dot clutched her chest. "Oh my gosh! You don't think Don squandered their life savings away, do you?"

"I hope not. Margaret still has the money from the coins and it's a substantial amount but still, that would be awful. She's going to call the bank and the investment companies linked to their retirement accounts tomorrow."

"I better get back inside," Dot said. "The extra income is nice but I'm getting too old for these late nighters."

Gloria felt guilty about eating at Dot's and adding to her burden but on the other hand, if everyone felt the same way, no one would eat at

Dot's and she'd have to close her doors. "Maybe you should consider hiring another full-time server or adding another employee to cover the busy breakfasts and dinners."

Dot reached for the screen door handle. "We are. It seems like these last few months business has really picked up. I don't know what Ray and I would've done if it hadn't been for Johnnie and Rose."

Gloria followed Dot into the kitchen and the acrid odor of burning food blasted her in the face. "Something's burning." Plumes of smoke seeped from the sides of the large commercial oven.

"It's the oven!" Dot darted to the oven and flung the door open.

Smoke poured out and Dot gasped. "It's a batch of dinner rolls." She grabbed a potholder sitting next to the oven, waved it in front of her face to clear the air and then reached inside to pull out the burnt bread.

"Oh my gosh!" Rose hurried into the kitchen. "I forgot all about those dinner rolls. I'm sorry Dot."

"It's okay. I should've been here to help."

"I'm going to get out of your hair." Gloria returned to the table where Paul was finishing his second helping of black-eyed peas and ham. He wiped his mouth, dropped the dirty napkin next to the empty plate and leaned back in his chair. "I'm sold. I tried to coax Rose into sharing the recipe but she refused."

"I guess we'll just have to come here to eat whenever you get a craving for Rose's black-eyed peas." Gloria reached for her purse sitting next to her chair. She was tempted to have Paul drive by Margaret's place but remembered Chad was there and didn't want to disturb them.

When they arrived back home, Paul made a beeline for his recliner. "Time for a nap." Mally, who followed them into the living room, waited patiently for Paul to get comfortable before she jumped onto the end of the recliner and crawled onto his lap.

Gloria settled into the other recliner. She grabbed her e-book reader and reading glasses flipping the cover open.

She'd recently started a murder mystery story and was near the middle of the book but the story had started to drag. Not only that, the main character was making some dumb mistakes. Gloria wanted to reach inside the story and shake some sense into her.

What sane person would drive to an abandoned house in the middle of the night where a body had been found the day before and not tell anyone where she was going? To top it off, Corinne, the main character, had forgotten and left her cell phone at home.

Aggravated, she shut the cover of the e-book reader, reached over and slipped the remote from Paul's hand. He stirred but didn't wake so she turned the volume down and began flipping through the channels.

Finally, she started to doze off when the late night news came on. Gloria gave up and wiggled out of her chair before nudging her husband's arm. "Paul, it's time for bed."

She let him use the bathroom first as she herded Mally outside for a final bathroom break before they all settled in for the night. After saying their prayers, Gloria rolled over to face the wall.

There was a chill in the air so she pulled the covers to her chin and snuggled deeper under the blankets. As Gloria drifted off to sleep listening to Paul's soft snores, her last thought was she hoped Margaret would be able to straighten out her finances and tomorrow would be less hectic than today had been.

If only she knew!

# Chapter 10

"Do you hear a noise?" Gloria, still half asleep, rolled over to face Paul.

Paul groaned. "It sounds like someone is pounding on the door." He flung the covers back, slid out of bed and stumbled to the door.

"You're going to answer the door dressed like that?" Gloria pointed at his boxer shorts and bare chest.

Paul glanced at his state of undress. "You're right."

"I'll go." Mally squeezed through the door and Gloria grabbed her robe on the way out. She picked up the pace as Mally, who had charged ahead, began barking her head off.

The pounding intensified. "I'm coming, I'm coming!"

Shadows filled the corners of the kitchen but it was still light enough for Gloria to get a clear view of the person peering in through the glass pane. It was her sister, Liz.

She flipped the deadbolt and jerked the door open. "What in the world are you doing here?" Gloria's gaze drifted from her sister's face to the large suitcase sitting next to her.

"I tried to call your cell phone late last night and early this morning to let you know I was on my way but you didn't answer," Liz said. "Aren't you going to invite me in?"

Gloria pushed the door open and stepped aside. She watched in disbelief as Liz tugged the large suitcase through the door and parked it in the middle of the kitchen floor.

"You called late last night? I was probably in bed," Gloria said. "Is everything all right?" There was no way Liz had driven over 1200 miles from Central Florida to West Michigan just to "pop in" for a visit.

Her eyes narrowed and she glanced out the window. Liz's sedan was parked in front of the garage. "You drove all the way up here by yourself? Where's Frances?" Frances was Liz's best friend. They had moved to Florida together, not long after Liz cashed in on her windfall from selling the "Aunt Ethel" coins.

Liz plopped down in the kitchen chair. "She's still in Florida. Her boyfriend, Harvey, moved in with her. She'll never come back to Michigan. The old fart has some bucks. Frances latched on to a real sugar daddy."

She shifted her gaze and eyed the empty coffee pot. "I could use a strong cup of black coffee right about now."

"I'd have made a pot if I'd known you were coming," Gloria said sarcastically as she stepped around Liz's suitcase. She filled the basket with coffee and added an extra scoop. It was going to be a long day.

"You still haven't told me what you're doing here and what on earth possessed you to drive halfway across the country to show up on my doorstep."

"I need some help," Liz said. "Are those donuts on top of your fridge?" She didn't wait for an answer as she sprung from the chair and headed to the fridge. She pulled the bakery box down and lifted the lid. "Is this all you've got? I don't like powdered sugar donuts."

Gloria frowned. "Beggars can't be choosers." The coffee finished brewing and Gloria poured two cups. She placed one of the cups in front of Liz, who was eating a donut she didn't like and sat across from her sister.

"What kind of help?" The sooner Gloria got to the bottom of Liz's surprise visit, the better.

"I'm having...financial difficulty."

Gloria had just taken a sip of coffee and started to choke. "You're kidding," she sputtered.

"I wish I was." Liz went on to explain how she'd hooked up with a pro golfer who worked at a local golf course near her home. According to Liz, he was a smooth talker with a penchant for expensive toys.

Gloria interrupted. "What kind of expensive toys?"

Liz shrugged. "The usual. A Porsche Macan, a Rolex watch, a Louis Vuitton custom golf bag."

"You bought him all that crap?" Gloria's eyes grew wide in disbelief.

Liz fiddled with the handle of the coffee cup. "Martin had an image to uphold, what with being a golf pro at the prestigious Royal Palm Plantation Country Club. Besides, he was hinting at proposing to me. What was I supposed to do?"

"Say no, Liz. Just say no."

"Say no to what?" Paul wandered into the kitchen. "Hello Liz." If Paul was surprised to see

Liz sitting at his kitchen table, he did a good job of hiding it.

"Hi Paul."

"Liz was just telling me she hooked up with a gigolo and she bought him a bunch of expensive gifts. I hope you didn't spend all your money on him."

The look on Liz's face told Gloria it was exactly what Liz had done. "You didn't..."

"Well." Liz had the decency to appear embarrassed. "Not *all* of it. I still have the house. I loaned him some money so he could drive to Poughkeepsie, New York to visit his dying mother."

Gloria rolled her eyes. "Liz! That's the oldest trick in the book. Let me guess...he's avoiding your phone calls."

"Not quite," Liz hedged. "His cell phone has been disconnected."

Gloria pounded her fist on the table causing Liz to jump.

"That's why I'm here," Liz whined. "I need you to help me track Martin down and get some of my money back."

"I think you should sell the place in Florida and move back up here where I can keep an eye on you."

"I can't." Liz lifted her coffee cup and took a sip. "I rented out my place. I used the deposit and first month's rent to get up here."

Gloria buried her head in her hands. "Elizabeth Applegate. You are the most irresponsible person I know."

Liz cut her off. "Spare the lecture, at least until after we track Martin down. Then you can lecture me all you want. In the meantime, I need a place to hang my hat."

"Green Springs has a very nice motel," Gloria said.

"Gloria," Paul chimed in. "Liz is your own flesh and blood."

"Another reason why I'm suggesting a hotel." Liz looked like she was ready to burst into tears and Gloria quickly caved. "Okay, but we need to set a date for your departure. You know the saying, 'Guests, like fish, begin to smell after a few days.'"

"I'll leave as soon as you help me track down Martin," Liz bargained.

"We're dealing with our own crisis," Gloria said.

Liz broke off a chunk of donut and began chewing. "Don't tell me you're having marital difficulties already." She shifted to face Paul. "I tried to warn you she's difficult to live with."

Gloria, near the breaking point with her sister, reached over and punched her in the arm. "You're already skating on thin ice, sister. Don't make me kick you out before you even unpack."

"I'm sorry," Liz apologized. "I didn't mean it."

"Don Hansen died," Gloria said.

"Don Hansen…you mean Margaret's husband?" Liz set the rest of her uneaten donut on her napkin. "She's probably set to come into some serious ka-ching. Maybe she'll loan me some money."

Gloria reached over to pop her sister in the arm again but Liz was too quick and she jerked back, out of her sister's reach.

"I was kidding," Liz said. "What happened?"

Gloria briefly explained the situation. "Chad is in town to help his mother so hopefully they get the financial mess straightened out today."

"I feel so bad for Margaret," Liz said. "What a terrible situation and to be questioned by the police. Surely they don't think Margaret had anything to do with Don's death."

Liz polished off the rest of her donut and stood. "I have one more suitcase to bring in."

Gloria waited until Liz had reached her car before turning to her husband. "I say we let Liz have the house and we move into a motel."

"She could stay at my farm," Paul offered. "It's empty now that Allie moved out."

"No." Gloria shook her head. "No way. I hate to say that I don't trust her, but I don't trust her not to trash your place."

Paul grabbed the carafe of coffee and refilled his wife's empty cup before filling his own. "Are you going to help Liz track down the golf pro?"

"Yes, and the sooner the better," Gloria said. "Maybe we'll get lucky and there's still some money left we can recoup."

After Liz unpacked, they ate a light breakfast.

Paul stood. "I better get going. I'm starting the security detail job today over at the art museum."

The local Green Springs Art Museum was receiving a shipment of valuable exhibit items from the ill-fated Titanic. The exhibit was a feather in the museum's cap and the museum's curator had lined up 24-hour security for the exhibit's ten-day event.

The exhibit would be moving to the larger Grand Rapids Art Museum after leaving Green Springs.

Gloria passed Liz on the porch as she walked Paul to his car. "I'll be home for dinner." He hugged and kissed his wife before opening the door and sliding behind the wheel.

He nodded his head toward the house. "Good luck."

"Thanks. I'll need it." Gloria wandered back inside. Liz was nowhere in sight although Gloria could hear her humming from the back of the house.

Mally trotted into the kitchen. Tied to each of her ears were bright red bows. "What in the world?"

Liz followed Mally into the kitchen. "I bought some velvet bows for Fifi, Martin's poodle, but never got to give them to her." Her lower lip began to quiver.

"Fifi?" Gloria had her doubts Martin even owned a dog. She'd already formed an opinion of the man who took her sister's money and it wasn't a pleasant one.

The quivering lip vanished. "So when can we start hunting for Martin?"

"Now." *The sooner the better.* Gloria grabbed a pad of paper and pen from her desk and joined Liz in the kitchen. "Tell me everything you know about Martin, if that's even his real name."

"Oh, it is," Liz said. "I've seen his driver's license."

"What if his license is a fake?" Gloria asked.

Liz blinked rapidly. "I hadn't thought of that, but I'm pretty sure that's his name. Martin Heemingstar." She spelled it out.

“It’s a unique name,” Gloria said. “If that’s his real name it will make our job easier.”

“And if he’s in Poughkeepsie,” Liz added. “He’s around 6’1” tall, blonde hair, a little on the shaggy side. He has a goatee and bright blue eyes. He has an amazing tan from spending all his time outside and he’s very muscular from swinging golf clubs all day.”

Gloria jotted some notes. “Age?”

“He’s thirty-nine but looks younger.”

Gloria dropped the pen. “Liz! I was only kidding about the gigolo thing but I take it back. You’re robbing the cradle!”

Liz squirmed in her chair. “I didn’t mean to. He was teaching me how to improve both my golf and tennis swing and one thing led to another.”

“I bet it did.” Gloria shook her head. “You said he told you he was heading to Poughkeepsie to visit his dying mother?”

"Yep. He called me right after he got there to tell me he made it safely. I haven't heard from him since."

Gloria tapped the end of the pen on top of the table. "Did he ask you to send more money?"

"Yes." Liz's look of discomfort grew. "I told him I didn't have any and that's the last time I heard from him."

"Do you know where he lives in Florida?"

"Yes. We spent all of our time at my place. We drove by his apartment once and I wanted to stop to, you know, check it out, but he said it was a mess and he would be embarrassed to show it to me."

"So you have no idea where he lives."

"I guess not," Liz admitted in a small voice. "The more we talk, the more foolish I look, like I've been taken."

"It happens all the time," Gloria said. "Unfortunately, this might be a very expensive lesson for you." She sucked in a deep breath. "Let's start with online searches. We can also call Royal Palm Plantation to see if they can provide any useful information."

"I already tried that," Liz said. "They said it's against company policy to tell me anything."

"My guess is if Martin Heemingstar is his real name and he hightailed it to Poughkeepsie, he's going to run out of money and will have to start looking for a job."

Liz finished Gloria's sentence. "At a local golf course. The swankier the better."

"Yep." Gloria's cell phone began to ring. It was Lucy.

"Hey Lucy."

"Hi Gloria. I'm sorry to bother you but we have a 911 crisis involving Margaret. Ruth is at work so we're having an emergency meeting behind the post office."

# Chapter 11

Gloria's heart sank. She had a feeling whatever it was had to do with Margaret and Don's retirement and bank accounts. "I'll..." She glanced at Liz across the table. "We'll be right there."

She disconnected the call and dropped the phone in her purse. "We're having an emergency Garden Girls meeting behind the post office. Do you want to go with me?"

"Of course," Liz popped out of her seat. "It will take my mind off my own problems."

The women hurried out of the house and Liz waited for Gloria to pull the car out of the garage before easing into the passenger seat. She reached for the seatbelt. "Won't the girls be surprised to see me?"

“They’ll be as shocked as I was,” Gloria muttered as she shifted into drive and swung Annabelle onto the road.

By the time they reached the back of the post office, Margaret, Dot, Lucy, Ruth and Andrea were already huddled near the dumpster.

“Liz?” Ruth stared at Liz. “What are you doing here?”

“It’s a long story.” Gloria shifted her purse to her other arm. “Don’t you have to keep an eye on the post office?”

“Kenny is covering for me but we have to hurry,” Ruth said. “He’s gotta head out for his route soon.” She turned to Margaret. “What happened?”

Margaret cleared her throat. “Chad and I got up first thing this morning and drove to the bank to straighten out the bank accounts. We also had two of our IRA’s at the bank so I figured I could take care of all three issues in person.”

She continued. “When we got there, George, the bank’s vice president and a personal friend of Don’s called us into his office and shut the door. I knew right then something was terribly wrong.”

Margaret stared at her folded hands as she fought to maintain her composure. Gloria patted her shoulder. “Take your time.”

“It’s gone.” Margaret looked up, her eyes brimming with unshed tears.

“What’s gone?” Lucy asked.

“All of the money in our retirement accounts. It appears Don forged my signature on my retirement accounts and cleaned them out.” Margaret fumbled with her purse latch, reached inside and pulled out a sheet of paper. She handed it to Gloria.

“There’s a couple hundred bucks in the retirement account. The savings account has less than fifty bucks.”

She continued. "If not for the money from the coins Don couldn't get his hands on, I'd be flat busted broke."

Gloria slipped her reading glasses on and studied the paper. "On Friday, June 12th there was a withdrawal. There was another one exactly two weeks later and a third one exactly three weeks later." She handed the paper to Margaret. "He did all this in the last few months."

"I'm shocked," Dot said.

"Me too," Ruth agreed. "What did he do with all the money?"

"I wish I knew." Margaret's hand trembled as she folded the piece of paper. "George swore up and down he had no idea, although he was able to give Chad and me one clue."

"What clue?" Andrea asked.

"When Don took out the money, he mentioned something about a big investment deal with one of the guys at the country club. Don told George he was going to double the money."

"Did George question Don if you were on board with the investment deal?" Gloria had a hard time believing the bank's vice president would let him walk away with that much cash without questioning it. Of course, the fact they were friends and the man had replaced Don may have swayed his decision, causing him to do something he wouldn't normally do.

"According to George he tried, but Don cut him off," Margaret said.

Gloria began to pace. "Perhaps the deal went bad. Don realized he'd lost all the money. He and the 'business partner' had a falling out at the country club which is where Don had his heart attack."

"If I lost that kind of money, I'd have a heart attack too," Liz said.

Gloria abruptly stopped. "You're in no position to judge," her sister reminded her.

Liz shrugged and began studying her fingernails. "Touché."

"Chad and you should confront the person, if you know who it is," Ruth said.

"We tried. We went from the bank to the country club to see if we could find anyone who knew what was going on. We found a couple of the other senior members. Although they seemed genuinely sorry to hear of Don's passing, they swore up and down they knew nothing about a business deal and couldn't even remember who all was involved in the incident on the golf course."

"Chad was able to squeeze out a name, though," Margaret said. "Ed Shields was one of them. Don and he were golfing partners. He was some hot shot private investor guru."

She went on to tell the group how Chad had tracked down Ed Shields and attempted to talk to him. He'd hung up on her son when he found out who he was.

Margaret shoved the paper into her purse. "Phil Holt, one of the owners of the golf club, told me he didn't want to talk, said it was bad for business and Don's death had nothing to do with Montbay Hills Golf & Country Club."

"In other words, don't start snooping around," Gloria said.

"Yeah. That's the impression Chad and I got. I have a feeling there's more to the story, something they're trying to cover up but I don't know how to prove it."

Liz, who had been silent, spoke. "I have an idea. What if Gloria and I go over there, do a little intel and see what we can find out?"

Margaret shook her head. "It's a member's-only golf club. You have to jump through hoops just to step foot on the property."

"Oh, there's a way around it." Liz turned to her sister. "My connections at Royal Palms Plantation Country Club might actually come in handy."

Margaret, familiar with all of the top country clubs in the United States, lifted a brow. "You know someone at Royal Palms?"

"You could say that," Liz said. "Leave it to me. I'll have a trial membership by tomorrow morning."

"What about us?" Lucy asked.

"Once I have the trial membership, I can invite guests to join me in the clubhouse, on the golf course or on the tennis courts," Liz said.

"I haven't played tennis in years," Gloria said.

Liz patted her sister's back. "You're never too old to pick it up again. If I didn't get anything else out of my relationship with Martin, I did learn to play a decent game of tennis and golf. We'll be on the tennis courts by noon tomorrow, guaranteed or you can throw me out of your house."

"Don't tempt me," Gloria joked. Her expression grew serious as she turned to

Margaret. "Have you started working on the funeral arrangements?"

Margaret nodded somberly. "Yes. Chad and I discussed it last night. It will be Thursday at 2:00 p.m. at Rolling Hills Funeral Home in Green Springs. I decided against a visitation. I just can't handle it."

"I better go." Margaret glanced at her watch. "Chad and I want to visit the cemetery to take a look at the family plot."

Margaret shuffled to her SUV and climbed in. Gloria's heart broke for her friend. Not only was she having to bury her husband, she was discovering he may have squandered their life savings and on top of all that, the police still hadn't cleared her name.

"Poor Margaret. If we can't get her money back, maybe we can at least clear her name and give her some closure on what exactly happened to Don. Something isn't adding up and I think at least one person at the country club knows something," Gloria said.

"I agree," Ruth said. "I'll keep my eyes and ears open here at the post office. Don's death has been the talk of the town all morning."

Liz turned to Andrea. "I'm sorry I missed your wedding. I bet you were a beautiful bride."

"She was," Gloria said. "I'm glad Brian and she decided to hold a ceremony and reception here in Belhaven. Niagara Falls ain't got nothin' on an old fashioned small town wedding."

"You got married in Niagara Falls?" Liz perked up. "You didn't happen to swing by Poughkeepsie, New York while you were there, did you?"

Gloria snorted. "We'll deal with your dilemma just as soon as we help Margaret."

"I know you will," Liz said. "I'm not leaving town until you do."

# Chapter 12

Gloria was chomping at the bit to do something to help poor Margaret and the next couple of days dragged by.  She was also dreading Don's funeral.

Surprisingly enough, Liz wasn't in Gloria's hair.  She was content to head out during the day, visiting friends who still lived in the nearby Dreamwood Retirement Community.

Gloria suspected her sister was up to something else, but she was being secretive with her telephone conversations and whenever Gloria caught her on the internet, she quickly closed out of whatever she was doing so her sister couldn't see.

Gloria offered to help Liz track down Martin but Liz had a sudden change of heart and didn't seem interested any longer.  She even went as far as to assure Gloria she would be leaving to return to Florida soon even if she wasn't able to track down Martin or her money.

When pressed, Liz finally confessed the rental was only for a month, which struck terror into Gloria's heart. A month of living with Liz was the same as a lifetime of living with Liz.

Paul didn't seem to mind either way. Of course, he was gone all day and the only time he saw Liz was in the evening and sometimes not even then if Liz was out running the roads.

Gloria talked to Margaret several times and it appeared the investigation into Don's death had stalled. Detective Givens was keeping the investigation open and the only thing he would tell Margaret was they were still following up on several leads.

Detective Givens was new to the local police force and Paul didn't know him so he wasn't able to get insider updates on the status. Gloria thought about calling Allie, Paul's daughter, who worked as a dispatcher at the Montbay County Sheriff Department but decided against it.

She would save calling on Allie for when she was in a real pinch for information. Gloria still hadn't started digging around into Don's suspicious death, partly because Margaret had her hands full with the funeral arrangements and finances and she didn't want to stick her nose in where it didn't belong.

In other words, there might be nothing to investigate. Don could have decided to swallow a bunch of pills to end his life and just to make sure he followed through, decided to start his car and sit inside his garage with it running after he passed out.

Gloria had started canning tomatoes from her garden and gingerly set the last jar on the kitchen towel when Liz breezed in, waving a piece of paper. "I've got it."

"Got what?"

"The invitation for trial membership at Montbay Hills," Liz said. "I had to pull a few strings at Royal Palms and Dreamwood's public golf course, but I finally got it."

"I need to talk to Margaret to see if she wants us snooping around," Gloria said. "The funeral is this afternoon."

Paul planned to work half a day at the museum and return home so he and Gloria could attend the funeral together.

"I almost forgot," Liz said. "Well, regardless, I'd like to check out the tennis courts, plus I need to practice my tennis swing." She clasped her hands and made a swinging motion. "You can go with me."

"I told you I haven't played tennis in years."

"It's like riding a bike. You'll pick it up fast."

"I suppose..." Liz had a point. If Paul and she decided to head south for the winters, she might like to take up tennis or even golf. They seemed to be among the more popular sports for retirees. "I suppose it wouldn't hurt."

Paul arrived right on time and after eating a quick lunch, he changed into his suit. Gloria slipped into a navy blue dress she'd recently purchased. Liz strolled into the kitchen wearing a bright cornflower-colored dress and sparkly purple pumps.

Gloria wrinkled her nose. "It looks like you're going to a party, not a funeral."

Liz straightened her neckline. "This is all I have. They don't sell drab colored clothing in Florida. Everything is bright and sunny."

"I'll loan you an outfit. Follow me." She motioned Liz to follow her to the master bedroom where she dug around inside her closet until she found a skirt and blouse that was more modest.

Liz emerged from the bathroom and Gloria crossed her arms as she inspected the outfit. "Much better."

"I feel like an old woman," Liz griped.

"You *are* an old woman."

Liz grumbled all the way to the kitchen and even after she climbed into the back seat of the car until Gloria gave her a warning look.

Liz knew she was treading on thin ice and quickly changed the subject. "I was thinking we could head over to the country club for a game of tennis tomorrow. It shouldn't be too busy on a Friday."

Paul gave his wife a quick glance. "You're taking up tennis?"

"Liz wants to practice her swing and decided to take me with her. She finagled a trial membership over at Montbay Hills Golf & Country Club."

"And it's only for a month." Liz leaned forward in her seat.

"You're not going to snoop around to find out who Don was arguing with shortly before his death, are you?"

"I hadn't planned on it," Gloria said. "Margaret hasn't asked me to."

"Good." Paul patted Gloria's hand. "Sometimes it's best to let things go. Margaret has enough on her mind right now."

Chad, Margaret's son, planned to leave the following morning. He needed to return home and to work. He attempted to convince his mother to go with him so she wouldn't be alone in the house but Margaret refused, insisting she had her friends to keep an eye on her.

The funeral home parking lot was full. Don had many acquaintances and friends from both his career at the bank and all the years he'd spent as a member of the country club.

Gloria briefly wondered if the man or men Don had argued with would be there. After parking, she followed Paul inside and Liz brought up the rear. She spotted Margaret standing next to her son, near the front of the closed casket.

The trio joined the end of the line to offer their condolences.

"I'm glad this is almost over," Margaret said as she hugged her friend.

"I know you are," Gloria whispered in her ear. "God will help you through this day and through the days ahead."

Margaret hugged Paul next and finally Liz. "I almost didn't recognize you in that outfit."

"This getup belongs to Gloria," Liz said. "She made me change."

Margaret gave her a half smile. "Thank you for coming."

The trio moved on and joined Lucy, Ruth, Dot and Ray, Rose and Johnnie as well as Andrea and Brian, who stood off to the side in a quiet alcove.

Lucy dabbed at her eyes. "This is so sad." Her eyes wandered to the casket. "It reminds me of James' and Gary's funerals."

"Me too." Gloria sighed. "I guess the older we get, the more funerals we're going to attend. It's just a part of life." The group discussed the graveside service, scheduled for immediately after the funeral. After the graveside service, Dot was hosting a reception or repass for family and friends at the restaurant.

All of the women had chipped in to cover the cost of the food. It would be a simple affair with comfort foods and a time of remembrance.

After the somber funeral, Ruth, Gloria, Dot, Rose, Andrea and Lucy caravanned to the restaurant to begin the meal preparations. The men had gone on to the graveside service to represent for their spouses.

Gloria transferred the garlic mashed potatoes from the large stainless steel pot to large serving bowls and placed them on the center island where Lucy picked them up and carried them to the long side tables they'd set up to hold the food.

There were also large trays of baked and fried chicken, meatballs, green beans, corn, freshly baked rolls and several cakes and pies the women had baked ahead of time.

They finished setting out the food, along with the dishes and silverware and guests began to file in. By the time Margaret arrived, the place was full of family and friends. There wasn't a single empty seat in the place. In fact, many of the guests lined the walls and stood eating.

Margaret took one look at all of the people who had shown up to show their love and support and burst into tears. Chad led his mother to the kitchen where Gloria and Dot were replenishing the platters of meat and rolls.

"Oh dear." Gloria wiped her hands on her apron and hurried to Margaret's side. The friends quickly circled Margaret and Gloria began to pray. "Dear Heavenly Father, Please give Margaret the comfort and peace that can only come from You. Lord, you know today is so difficult for her. We ask that you wrap your arms around her and hold her close."

Gloria's voice cracked and she began to sob.

"Amen," Lucy whispered before bursting into tears. The women began to bawl. Ray, who had jumped in to help, took one look at the kitchen full of crying women, walked out of the room and returned with several boxes of Kleenex.

Paul arrived, as did Johnnie, Brian and Lucy's on-again, off-again boyfriend, Max. Chad comforted his mother and then returned to the dining room to speak with the guests.

"We'll take over." The men shooed the women to the picnic table out back and took over hosting the reception.

"I'm sorry Margaret," Gloria whispered. "We were supposed to be strong for you."

"It's okay." Margaret grabbed a tissue and loudly blew her nose. "I just love you all so much. You have no idea how much your support and love means to me." She eyed Dot. "I may have to hit you up for a job now that I'm flat broke and Don has left me with this mess."

"You haven't recovered any of the money?" Rose asked.

"No. The bank and retirement accounts are still active but there's only enough money in each one to keep them open. I might have a thousand dollars total if you add all the money together."

"Except for the money from the coins," Gloria said.

"Yes. I still have the money from the coins. Thank the Lord I have no debt. If I'm careful the money will last," Margaret said. "Chad is going to research some safe investments with the highest return possible to try to add to my nest egg."

Margaret reached for another tissue, dabbed her eyes and began twisting it around her finger. "Chad went to the country club to try to find out what happened. You know, who Don may have been involved with that had something to do with our money and Phil Holt stonewalled him again."

Liz wandered outside to join the women. "If you don't mind me asking, how much money are we talking about?"

"Liz!" Gloria gasped.

"It's okay." Margaret waved a hand. "Let's just say it was more than a million."

"A million bucks?" Liz's eyes widened. "Whew! I'd be all over that. No way would I let someone rip me off."

"You mean like Martin?" Gloria asked pointedly.

"I'm working in recouping my money," Liz said. She turned to Margaret. "Have you thought about letting Gloria do a little digging around at the country club?"

Margaret glanced at Gloria. "I didn't want to ask since you have you hands full right now."

"With Liz," Gloria pointed out. "I'm willing to do whatever I can to help, Margaret. If you want me to do a little poking around at the country club, I'll be happy to give it a shot."

Liz placed the palms of her hands on the edge of the table and leaned forward. "I finagled a trial membership at Montbay Hills. I was trying to talk Gloria into running over there tomorrow so I can practice my tennis swing."

"I think it's an excellent idea," Dot said. "If anyone can sniff out the money, it will be Gloria."

"I agree," Andrea said.

"I dunno." Gloria gazed at Margaret hesitantly. "Are you sure?"

"If you're willing, I'd appreciate it," Margaret said.

“The sooner the better,” Ruth said. “If you wait too long the trail will grow cold.”

“And the money will be gone,” Rose added.

“It’s settled,” Liz said. “We’ll head over there tomorrow morning to start our recon mission.”

# Chapter 13

"There's a spot." Gloria pointed to an empty parking spot near the center of the Montbay Hills Golf & Country Club parking lot.

"Way out there? No way. We're VIP baby." Liz kept going and drove her sedan into the parking spot marked *guest parking*. "It was like pulling teeth to get this trial membership and I plan to take full advantage of it."

They exited the car and made their way to the door on the far side of the building. "We're looking for Robert West, he's the sales director." Liz stopped abruptly and reached for the handle. "I had to spring for a 30-day trial membership but it will only cost you $500 bucks."

"Cost *me* five hundred bucks?" Gloria tightened her grip on her purse. "You're telling me *I* have to pay?"

"Of course," Liz said calmly. "You can't expect them to let us play at this beautiful club and use their tennis courts without paying for it."

"But..." To Gloria, five hundred dollars seemed like a whole lot of money just to whack a small yellow ball across a net.

"You know I'm broke," Liz argued. "Plus, this is a bargain. You wouldn't believe what they charge at Royal Palm Plantations for a club membership." She didn't wait for her sister to answer as she opened the door and held it. "After you."

The inside of the office was masculine, the walls covered in a rich mahogany paneling. The smell of freshly cut grass followed them into the spacious shop and Gloria trailed behind her sister as she made her way to the counter in the back.

"Yes. I'm Liz Applegate. I'm here to see Robert West about my membership and to remind him we plan to try out the tennis courts today."

The young man behind the counter nodded. "I'll go track Mr. West down." He disappeared through an open door and returned moments later, followed by a tall man with a crew cut and thick black glasses. "Ms. Applegate?"

"That's me." Liz took a step forward.

"I have your paperwork here." Robert West briefly explained the country club's policies on the use of the tennis courts, the exercise room, the golf course, golf carts, the green fees, the rental of golf clubs and other details Gloria tuned out.

"I'll need the five hundred dollars for your thirty-day trial membership."

Liz stepped aside and motioned Gloria to the counter.

"Highway robbery," Gloria muttered under her breath. She frowned at the man. "Do I get a refund if we decide within the thirty-day period we don't want to join?"

"Unfortunately not. The fee is non-refundable." The man slid the papers across the counter for Gloria to look them over. "The policy on a *90-day* trial is typically strictly enforced. We only agreed to a 30-day trial period since it's nearing the end of the season."

"Lucky us," Gloria said as she glared at Liz.

She signed her name, handed him her credit card and waited for him to complete the transaction. After signing the slip of paper, she tucked the extra copy in her purse. "I'll have fun explaining this one to Paul."

"I set aside our Babolat Pure tennis rackets for you to try along with a new can of tennis balls." Mr. West reached under the counter and set a touch card on the counter. "I even threw in a thirty dollar gift card for Whispering Oaks Restaurant. The hours are on the back."

Liz snatched the gift card off the counter and shoved it in her front pocket. “How kind of you.”

“Follow me.” The man stepped from behind the counter and Liz and Gloria followed him outside, down the sidewalk and around the corner.

“The tennis courts are down this path about a quarter of a mile. You can’t miss them.” He pointed to a two-seater golf cart sitting next to the building. “It’s a distance so I thought I would loan you one of our carts.”

“I’ll drive.” Liz handed the tennis rackets and can of balls to Gloria before she hurried to the driver’s side and hopped behind the wheel.

Gloria frowned as she slid in the passenger seat. “Where’s the seatbelt?”

Robert West began to explain how to operate the golf cart and Liz held up a hand. “I have a golf cart at my home in Florida.”

"Good." Mr. West took a step back and gazed up at the clear blue skies. "It's going to be a beautiful day to play tennis. I hope you enjoy your game of tennis."

"Thanks." Liz took her foot off the brake and the cart coasted onto the paved path. "I already checked out the layout of the club grounds so I know which way to go."

"This isn't just a fun day out, Liz. Remember the reason we're here is to try to glean some information about the incident with Don the day he suffered his heart attack."

"True, but all work and no play makes for a dull Gloria," Liz quipped as she stopped the cart in the small gravel parking lot in front of the tennis courts and climbed out. "What's the gate code?"

"What gate code?" Gloria carried her purse, both tennis rackets and the can of balls to the gate.

"The one he wrote on the paper you put in your purse."

Gloria fumbled inside her purse for the piece of paper and pulled it out. "One five one one."

"One five one one." Liz repeated the numbers as she pressed the buttons. The lock clicked and she pushed the metal gate open. "Bingo."

Gloria trudged through the open door and stared at the double courts. "I can't believe I'm doing this."

Liz ignored her sister as she reached for a tennis racket. "I'll use this one." She grabbed the can of balls from Gloria, popped the top and pulled one out. "I'll take the duce court."

"Duce court?"

"The right service court," Liz explained. "You go on the other side."

Gloria walked to the other side of the net, tennis racket in hand.

"Keep an eye on the ball." Liz lightly tossed the ball in the air and hit it dead center. *Whack!*

The ball sailed through the air, aimed right toward Gloria's head and she ducked.

"What are you doing?" Liz hollered.

"Ducking," Gloria said.

"You're supposed to hit the ball, not duck from it."

Gloria hurried to the back of the court to retrieve the ball. "Maybe if you hadn't tried to hit me with it, I would've taken a swing." She lifted her tennis racket, tossed the ball and swung. She missed the ball and it bounced on the clay court.

"Nice shot...not!" Liz taunted.

Gloria glared at her sister. "I told you I haven't played tennis in years."

"Let me give you a couple pointers." Liz strode to the center net. "Stance is everything. Make sure to keep your eye on the ball."

Gloria nodded and picked up the ball. This time, she hit the ball dead center and it whizzed through the air, across the net where Liz hustled and then swung, hitting the ball back across the net.

Gloria missed on the return but after a few more attempts, was able to hit the ball half the time, which she considered a success. Gloria didn't plan to admit to Liz she was enjoying the tennis game.

It was a picture-perfect late summer afternoon and a light breeze fanned Gloria's face. "I should have brought one of those thingies to shade my eyes." She lowered her tennis racket. "I think I've had enough for today. Let's explore the rest of the club, especially the golf course."

They exited the court and Gloria pulled the gate shut behind her. "You're a pretty good tennis player."

"I'm not as proficient as I'd like to be, but it is good exercise and fun," Liz said. "I convinced

Frances to try it once. That's where she hooked up with her beau, Harvey. It was the first and last time she played."

They climbed back into the golf cart, zipped past the first nine holes and zigzagged through a cluster of towering oaks. When they cleared the trees, Gloria spotted a small concession stand, the Snack Shack, on the other side. "I'm ready for a break if you are. Let's check this place out."

Liz pulled the golf cart into the golf cart parking lot. "Me too. We should've brought some drinks with us. We'll remember next time."

The women exited the cart and headed to the counter. There was a small sitting area inside and the place was full of men. All eyes turned to the women as they stepped inside and over to the small counter.

Gloria perused the overhead menu board. "I'll have a bottled water and hot dog please."

"Make it two," Liz said.

The man behind the counter rang up the purchases. "That'll be twelve dollars and forty-nine cents."

Gloria looked at Liz who shrugged her shoulders. "I'm broke."

"And you're beginning to sound like a broken record." Gloria reached inside her purse, pulled out her wallet and handed the man a ten and five. "Keep the change."

After they grabbed their bottled waters and hot dogs, they sat at a small corner table a couple had just vacated. Gloria wiped the crumbs off the table with a paper napkin and then opened her bottle of water.

After the women prayed, Gloria bit the end of her hotdog and studied the men seated inside. She wondered if any of them was Ed Shields, one of the men who had been golfing with Don the day of his heart attack.

She tried to eavesdrop on the group seated nearby but it was a dull conversation about golf swings and the upcoming golf tournament. One of the men was contemplating purchasing a new set of clubs.

Her mind drifted but she snapped back to attention when she caught the word funeral.

"My hotdog tastes rubbery," Liz complained.

Gloria held up a finger to silence her as she tilted her head in an attempt to hear the men talk.

"I was surprised Bolton had the nerve to show his face at the funeral home. Margaret should've tossed him out on his ear," one of the men said.

"I think it was all a misunderstanding." The man sitting across from him spoke. "If I were Margaret, I would've been more upset with Don. Heard he left her darn near destitute. I'm sure glad I didn't get caught up in the get-rich-quick scheme they were pedaling."

# Chapter 14

"Phil Holt should've revoked both Bolton and Ed's club membership," the first man said.

Gloria couldn't help herself. She spun around on the bench seat and faced the men. "I couldn't help but overhear your conversation. I'm an acquaintance of the Hansens. Don was involved in a money scheme?"

The man's eyes widened. "I-uh. It was just a rumor. We don't know for sure. Pure speculation."

"What if there is some truth to it?" Gloria insisted.

The men abruptly stood and one of them tossed some dollar bills on the table. "Like he said, it's just a rumor."

Liz, seeing their opportunity to gain a little information, sprang from her seat and hurried around the table. "I'm sure there are plenty of members here who heard the rumor. Who are Bolton and Ed?"

"I don't think..." The younger of the two men started to shake his head.

"Please?" Liz clasped her hands to her chest.

The other man shrugged. "She's right. It's not like no one else knows." He lowered his voice. "One of them is Nolan Bolton and the other one is Ed Shields. Don was the third wheel. I'm not sure on the fourth one. We've heard a couple names thrown out there."

"I appreciate the information." Liz lightly touched the older man's arm.

"You're new," he said as he eyed her with interest.

"Yes. We just joined with a trial membership," Liz explained. "But I won't be staying on. I live in Florida."

She chatted with the men a few more minutes while Gloria grabbed her cell phone and sent herself a message listing the men's names. After saving the message, she dropped her phone back inside her purse.

"There's a golf tournament Sunday and a big shindig over at the clubhouse for members. Montbay Hills pulls out all the stops and it's a swanky party. The tournament starts at 7:30 in the morning and the invitation-only party starts at four."

"The party sounds lovely but we don't have invites," Liz pouted.

The older man held up his hand. "No invitation needed. If you'd like to come, all you have to do is tell them is Rex invited you."

"Rex." Liz repeated his name. "Thank you so much Rex. Why all this hospitality makes me think I should be livin' in Michigan again."

The men exited the building. Rex looked back and Liz gave him a friendly wave.

"So long Martin," Gloria teased.

"Martin?"

"Like I said, so long Martin."

Liz took a big swig of water and replaced the cap. "This is strictly research. That man...Rex, was too old for me."

"He's our age," Gloria pointed out.

"Like I said, he's too old." Liz glanced at her watch. "Let's finish our tour of the grounds."

Liz put the pedal to the metal as they zipped around the rest of the golf course, took a drive by the golf club rental stand, the pool and spa area. Gloria suspected her sister was in a big hurry to finish the tour, hoping to 'run into' her new friend, Rex, back at the clubhouse.

By the time they finished their tour, the brutal round of tennis had caught up with Gloria. Her back was stiff and her knees ached, but it was a good soreness. It reminded her she was still alive, still kicking.

After they returned the tennis rackets and tennis balls to the office, they headed to Liz's car. "We are going to the party, right?"

Gloria was on the fence. On the one hand, the party would literally help them get their foot in the door. She was certain the get-rich-quick "schemers" were regulars. Rex had called them by name. She was also certain there was no way the suspects...err, men would miss one of the country club's premier party events.

"Yeah. I'm not sure I want to stand on the sidelines and watch a bunch of men try to hit a golf ball but the party would be the perfect opportunity to get to know some of the other members and hopefully uncover more information on the Ponzi scheme."

"I agree." Liz shifted the car in reverse and peered into her rearview mirror. "Rex mentioned there were four of them possibly involved. I wonder who the fourth person is."

Gloria shrugged. "Hard telling. Maybe he knew and didn't want to incriminate someone."

"Maybe it was one of the owners of the country club," Liz theorized. "An owner would be the last person you would want to point fingers at."

"True."

Liz stomped on the brake and Gloria lurched forward. "Easy on the brakes."

"Sorry. I thought I saw a furry rodent in the road," Liz said. "So we're on the lookout for Neal somebody."

Gloria pulled her cell phone from her purse and turned it on. "Nolan Bolton and Ed Shields."

"Right," Liz nodded. "It's going to be tough figuring out who we're looking for at the party."

"I've already given it some thought," Gloria said. "We can do an online search on social media. Ten bucks says there's a public page for Montbay Hills Golf & Country Club and if they post pictures and tag people, I suspect we might get lucky and be able to get a visual."

"Good idea," Liz said. "I never would've thought of that."

Paul still hadn't arrived home when Liz pulled the car into the drive. She parked close to the barn.

"Why don't you pull on the other side of the garage?" Gloria asked.

Liz wrinkled her nose. "Your trees are making a mess out of my car."

"Whatever." Gloria rolled her eyes. When they got inside, Gloria made a beeline for the computer. She turned it on and while she waited for it to warm up, she led Mally outside.

Mally disappeared around the side of the barn and when she didn't come back, Gloria followed after her and found her sniffing a pile of compost behind one of the storage sheds. "C'mon. It's time to go in."

Mally glanced at Gloria and then promptly trotted off in the opposite direction.

"You stinker!" Gloria followed Mally, who tore off across the yard and led Gloria on a merry chase back and forth. When she tired of the game, the pooch headed for the porch where she flopped down in front of one of the rocking chairs.

"Naughty dog," Gloria scolded when she caught up.

Mally hung her head and let out a low whine as Gloria held the door.

"Bingo. We got a hit." Liz hollered from the dining room.

Gloria grabbed her reading glasses from the kitchen table and joined her sister as she peered over Liz's shoulder. "There's Don." Liz pointed at the screen. "Someone tagged the others." Gloria read the names *Nolan Bolton, Ed Shields, Don Hansen and Becky Stone.*

"Becky Stone." Gloria squinted her eyes. "A woman. Look at the date of the picture. It was right around the time of Don's confrontation. I'll ask Margaret for the list of players Don played with."

She picked up her phone, texted Margaret and then snatched a notebook from the bin on the desk. "We need to get close to some of Don's golfing buddies. Someone knows something."

"Maybe it was someone from his banking years," Liz said. "Or maybe Don was the ringleader and started the Ponzi scheme, took the wrong person's money and they took him out."

Gloria wandered over to the dining room window and stared out. "All we know for certain is that Don did something with their retirement money. Rumors are flying at the golf course that Don was involved in a money aka Ponzi scheme, he got in an argument on the golf course which triggered his heart attack and the investigators are suspicious of Don's death. All the clues point to the country club."

"Which is why we need to be at their big blowout!" Liz said. "Once we have a list of Don's golfing buddies, we can start digging for dirt. I'm sure they will all be at the party if it's the event of the year that Rex claims it is."

"I think I'll give Margaret a call to see if she has time to stop by." Gloria vividly remembered the days following James' death and his funeral. Once the calls and visitors stopped, she was filled with an overwhelming sense of isolation. If not for her close group of friends, she wasn't sure what she would've done.

God was by her side during those dark days but he also sent her friends to be by her side to help her through.

Her call to Margaret went to voice mail and she still hadn't replied with the list of golf buddies. A small warning bell went off in Gloria's head. "I think I'll hop in the car and run by Margaret's place." She headed to the kitchen.

"We need to get Margaret out of the house," she continued. Gloria picked up her car keys and tossed them to Liz, who had followed her into the kitchen.

When they reached Margaret's place, her car was nowhere in sight. She didn't answer the door so Gloria retraced her steps and climbed back inside the car. "I don't think she's home."

A small flutter of the living room curtain caught Gloria's attention. "Or she's avoiding everyone." She fired off a text to her friend. *I'm concerned about you. I'd like to have you over for brunch tomorrow morning around ten. I'll pick you up.* Gloria read the text to Liz before pressing the send button.

"What if she refuses?" Liz asked as she backed out of the drive.

"I'll drag her out if I have to."

# Chapter 15

Liz and Gloria swung by Dot's Restaurant to invite Dot and Rose to the brunch. Their next stop was the post office. Ruth promised she would try to make it but it would depend on Kenny and how much mail they had to process first thing in the morning.

Next on the list was Lucy. She wasn't home either so Gloria texted her. Andrea was the only other person Gloria hadn't tried. "I would ask Andrea but she's technically still on her honeymoon and I hate to bother her."

Paul arrived home before Liz and Gloria. He'd called his wife before he left work, offering to pick up some fast food but Gloria felt guilty so she told him she would whip up a quick meal when he got there.

The "quick" meal ended up being tacos. Liz helped shred the lettuce and chop the tomatoes and onion while she cooked the meat on the stovetop. Alice had shared her "secret" taco-seasoning recipe with Gloria, not to be confused with her spicy "love potion," and Gloria was hooked.

She used the flavorful seasoning on tacos, burritos, homemade soups and dips. It beat the pre-packaged store brands hands down since it didn't contain any of the preservatives and chemicals the packets sold in the grocery stores. She used it all the time and had started making triple batches so she would always have the seasoning on hand.

Liz, who had finished chopping the vegetables, wandered over to the stove and sniffed appreciatively. "Is this the special taco seasoning you keep raving about?"

"It is." The meat finished cooking and Gloria added more spice plus a cup of tap water and then covered the pan to let it finish simmering.

Paul stepped into the kitchen and hungrily eyed the array of crisp taco shells and bowls of toppings. "Tacos...my favorite."

Liz placed a small pile of silverware on the table. "Gloria has been raving about this taco seasoning and wanted me to try it."

"I've been asking for homemade tacos for weeks now." Paul kicked his shoes off and tucked them in the corner of the shoe tray. "I guess we have to have company to get the good stuff."

Gloria playfully popped her husband in the arm and set the bowl of seasoned ground beef on the table. "You know that's not true."

Paul snaked his arm around his wife's waist and pulled her close before kissing her soundly. "I'm teasing. So what were you two up to today?"

"Tennis."

“Tennis?” Paul released his hold on his wife.

“Liz signed us up for a 30-day trial at Montbay Hills so we went there today. It was kinda fun,” Gloria admitted.

“Let me guess. You were also there to see what you could find out about Don’s incident on the golf course before his death.”

“A little,” Gloria hedged. “Margaret said she didn’t mind. Speaking of Margaret, we stopped by there earlier. No one answered the door but I could’ve sworn I saw a curtain move.”

“She’s in mourning,” Paul said. “It’s only been a few days since Don’s death and his funeral was yesterday. She’s probably still trying to come to grips with her loss.”

“I’m concerned because she’s all alone now that Chad left to go home.” Gloria slid into a chair and rested her chin on her fist. “I invited her and the other girls to brunch tomorrow to try to get her out of the house.”

"Montbay Hills is having a golf tournament this Sunday," Liz said. "There's a lavish party planned at the clubhouse after the tournament and we've been invited."

Paul lifted a brow as he eased into the chair next to his wife. "You're going?"

"I'm thinking about it," Gloria said. "If you don't mind, of course. Do you want to go?" It hadn't dawned on her to ask Paul if he wanted to go.

Paul glanced at Liz and then shifted his gaze to his wife. "I think I'll pass. You know I don't like stuffy parties, although I probably should go so I can keep an eye on you to keep you out of trouble."

"Me...get in trouble?" Gloria lifted her eyebrows innocently. "We've already paid for a trial membership so we might as well take advantage of the perks."

"We?" Paul asked. "Who are *we*?"

Liz had the good graces to look guilty. "I...was able to get a 30-day trial membership, which was a great deal since country clubs typically require 90-day trial periods."

"And she didn't have the money to pay the $500 fee so I paid," Gloria added.

Paul, who had taken a sip of his iced tea, spit it out. "Five hundred dollars? To hit a little ball across a net or onto some green grass?" he sputtered.

"Five hundred bucks is a bargain," Liz said calmly. "You wouldn't believe what they charge in Florida."

"I don't want to know what they charge in Florida," Paul gasped. He turned to his wife. "Did you really spend five hundred dollars?"

Gloria's face reddened at Paul's rant over the cost of the membership.

"I'm sorry," she said in a small voice. "I had no idea you would be this upset."

Paul, realizing he was blustering on in front of Liz, forced himself to take a deep breath. He reached over and patted Gloria's hand. "No, I should be the one to apologize. I'm just shocked you spent that kind of money on a frivolous activity."

"Frivolous," Liz said. "It's therapeutic. Some of the most successful people in the world spend a small fortune golfing."

"I'll go there tomorrow and ask for a refund," Gloria said quietly.

"No you won't." Paul shook his head. "I should have kept my mouth shut. You're an adult. If you want to buy a country club membership and you enjoyed playing tennis or want to give golf a try, then I'm all for it. I'll even go with you one day before the trial membership runs out."

"You will?" Gloria brightened.

"Yeah," Paul said, "but I won't be going to the party. You're on your own." He pointed at the heaping bowl of taco meat. "Now let's eat."

Despite starting dinner on a rocky note, they had a lively discussion of Liz telling Paul about Gloria's first tennis playing attempt. He, in turn, shared stories of his busy day, overseeing the delivery of the local museum's loaned artifacts. "We need to visit the exhibit before it ends."

"I would love to," Gloria said. "Maybe one day next week, after they finish setting up and the exhibit officially opens."

Liz offered to clean up after dinner, while Gloria called each of the girls to confirm the brunch time. Margaret was her last call and the call went to voice mail. She texted Andrea, who promised to run past Margaret's house to make sure their friend, was all right. Andrea told her if anything was wrong, she would call her. Otherwise, she would see her in the morning.

"You don't have to come, Andrea. I just didn't want to leave you out. Brian might want you to stay home with him."

Andrea told her the brief honeymoon was over and Brian was returning to work at Nails and Knobs, his hardware store in Belhaven, the following morning. She explained how she planned to take over the bookkeeping for all of Brian's businesses not to mention help him with inventory, stocking and some of the other day-to-day operations.

The newlyweds still hadn't decided what to do with each of their homes. Andrea was attached to her mini-mansion while Brian was attached to his modern lakefront home. The home had belonged to his grandparents and they had willed it to him when they died. He'd meticulously renovated the place and it was stunning.

After talking to each of the friends and leaving messages, Gloria began working on the breakfast brunch bake. The recipe called for it to sit overnight inside the fridge before she baked it in the oven the next morning.

Dot offered to bring a box of assorted donuts and bagels as well as some cooked slices of bacon. Andrea invited Alice who offered to bring torrijas, a Spanish bread pudding.

After wrapping up the brunch plans, Gloria wandered aimlessly around the house as she worried about Margaret.

Liz vanished inside her room where Gloria could hear the faint thump of music while Paul worked on the home computer.

On her third pass through the dining room, Paul stopped her. "You're nervous as a tick. Why don't we take a ride and check on the farm?" He slid the chair back and stood.

"Yeah. I'm restless. A ride might help." She tapped on Liz's door and told her they were going out for a drive.

The air was cool, the humidity of the day gone as they walked to Paul's car. Mally, not wanting to be left behind, followed them out.

Paul patted the dog's head. "You want to go for a ride to check on the farm?"

Mally's back half wiggled as she wagged her tail and then darted off across the yard. She looked back as if to say "hurry up" and then as soon as Gloria opened the rear door of the car, she jumped in.

"Mally, are you ready to go for a ride?" Gloria smiled at her pooch as she circled the backseat and flopped down.

Gloria climbed in the passenger seat and scooched across the seat until she was sitting in the middle, right next to Paul. "What's this?" He grinned as he reached for his seatbelt.

"It's me coming over here to be close to you." Gloria smiled and snuggled close. She instantly thought of Margaret, how she was alone now.

Alone and overwhelmed by what had happened. Her smile quickly faded.

They took their time driving to Paul's farm. The backroads were deserted and it was a welcome change for Gloria to be able to enjoy the view as she rode.

Paul's farm was similar in size to Gloria's farm. They hadn't stayed there since Allie moved out.

The old farmhouse was in need of renovations and mechanical updates but since no one was living in it for the most part, it didn't make sense to sink money into a home that sat empty. It was a shame.

Paul pulled the car into the circular drive and parked in front of the house. Gloria exited the car and held the door so Mally could scamper out. She promptly trotted over to the barn silos to investigate. After inspecting the silos, she patrolled the outside of the barn.

The round corncrib was next. The wooden slats near the bottom of the corncrib were missing and Mally slipped inside the empty bin to explore.

Gloria and Paul wandered over. "I wonder what happened to the bottom slats. C'mon Mally." Paul coaxed the pooch out. "I need to get those boards replaced to keep critters from moving in."

They wandered toward the back of the house and up the rear steps. Paul unlocked the door and led the way inside. He checked the entire house before turning the thermostat off. "No sense in wasting electricity."

"We can spend this weekend over here if you like," Gloria offered, a twinge of guilt prodding her. "Liz will watch my place."

"There's no cable television," Paul reminded her. "Or internet."

"True," Gloria said. "But you still have the old television antenna hooked up. We can sit around and read books or work on a puzzle or something…"

"Or enjoy each other's company." Paul's eyes twinkled as he teased his wife.

"Of course." Gloria batted her eyes flirtatiously before she made her way to the enclosed front porch. The porch was similar to the one on the front of Gloria's farmhouse but unlike Gloria's farm, there were no neighbors within sight, just acre after acre of farm fields as far as the eye could see.

They walked around the front and rear yards before finally heading back to the car for the ride home. The exercise from swinging the tennis racket not to mention squatting and bending her knees was catching up with Gloria. She rubbed the tops of her legs.

Paul cast a quick glance at her. "Are you okay?"

"My leg muscles are not used to chasing after tennis balls," she said. Back at the house, it took her a couple extra moments to coax her sore legs to move and she gingerly limped up the porch steps. "A hot bath sounds good."

After cashing in the coins from Aunt Ethel's farm, Gloria had splurged and completely renovated her bathroom, installing a larger single sink vanity, a new toilet and her favorite purchase, a large, jetted tub.

She headed to the bedroom to grab a pair of sweatpants and t-shirt and passed by the bathroom. The door was closed and she could hear Liz on the other side, singing.

"Looks like someone beat you to it." Paul pointed at the door.

Gloria frowned. "She's starting to cramp my style."

Paul followed his slow-moving wife into the living room and watched her ease into the nearby recliner. "How much longer is she staying?"

"I have no idea. She told me she has short-term tenants in her home. I thought her plan was to track down her golf pro/tennis pro/gigolo boyfriend but she seems to have lost interest."

The conversation stopped abruptly as Liz emerged from the bathroom and breezed into the living room. "You're back. That was not a very relaxing bath. I ran out of hot water halfway through. You must have one of those rinky-dink hot water tanks."

"Rinky-dink hot water tank?" Gloria exploded in a mini rant. Paul shook his head and hurried from the room. "I think I'll stay out of this one."

Mally lowered her ears and crawled under the coffee table.

"I've taken plenty of baths in my jetted tub and never run out of water."

"Huh." Liz sniffed. "Well, maybe it's on the fritz. The water was lukewarm at best. It also has a strong sulfur odor and now I feel scratchy all over."

To demonstrate, Liz started scratching her upper arms. "You probably need a water softener. These old farms don't have the best plumbing."

Gloria started to climb out of the recliner, a look of murder in her eyes.

"It's just a suggestion." Liz quickly retreated to her bedroom. "The bathroom is all yours," she hollered back.

Gloria climbed out of the chair and headed to the kitchen where she found Paul snacking on a bowl of mixed nuts and working on a crossword puzzle. "She'll be gone before you know it."

"Not soon enough." Gloria shuffled to the bathroom. Her mood darkened when she turned the faucet full force hot and stuck her hand under the lukewarm water.

"Dear God. Please give me patience to survive Liz's visit." She muttered a quick prayer before climbing into the tepid tub.

Despite her aggravation, Gloria closed her eyes and focused on all of her blessings, something she hadn't done in a while. By the time she finished her bath, her mood had improved.

She passed through the living room where Paul was watching television. "I'm still stiff and Liz used all of the hot water but at least I have a roof over my head, a husband I adore and food on the table."

"Good girl. Always count your blessings." Paul shifted in his recliner. "I'll be in after my show ends."

Gloria nodded and hobbled to the bedroom. She slipped into her pajamas and crawled into bed where she prayed God would help her appreciate and embrace her sister's annoying traits. As soon as she closed her eyes, she drifted off to sleep.

# Chapter 16

Dot glanced at the clock above Gloria's kitchen sink. "How much longer should we give her?"

"Five minutes," Gloria said. "If Margaret doesn't show up in the next five minutes, I'll drive to her house." She glanced out the window. "Ah. There's Ruth. Kenny must have covered for her at the post office." She stepped onto the porch and waited for Ruth to park her 'spy-mobile' behind Dot's van.

*Spy-mobile* was the nickname the friends had given Ruth's tricked out, bulletproof, video recording, surveillance center on wheels.

Ruth slid out of the van and hurried across the drive. "Margaret isn't here yet?"

"No." A movement caught Gloria's attention. "There she is now."

Margaret's SUV swung into the drive and came to an abrupt halt behind Lucy's jeep.

"I'll wait inside." Ruth headed into the kitchen while Gloria headed down the steps. She met Margaret by the driver's side of the SUV, opened the door and then took a step back as she studied the dark circles under her friend's eyes.

"I was just about to head out to track you down," Gloria said as she watched her friend ease out of the vehicle.

"I almost didn't come," Margaret admitted. "But I knew if I didn't you'd be on my doorstep." She glanced at the other vehicles parked in the drive. "Who all is coming to your brunch?"

Gloria rattled off the list. "Dot and Rose are already here. Ruth just arrived. Lucy is here. Liz is here."

Margaret interrupted. "I forgot about Liz. How's it going?"

Gloria groaned. "She's driving me up the wall but other than that, she's still alive."

Margaret chuckled. "I'd offer to let you ship her to my house but I'm not sure I'm up for a dose of Liz."

"I wouldn't send her to Sally Keane's place." Sally was a Belhaven resident. Gloria had had ups and downs with the woman. She was a constant complainer and now that she was semi-engaged and semi-dating Officer Nelson, she'd determined it was her duty to stick her nose into everyone else's business.

"Andrea and Alice should be here any second," Gloria said. "How are you?"

Margaret sucked in a breath, closed her eyes and nodded. "I'm hanging in there. Last night was rough. I barely slept. It was weird being in the house by myself. I kept hearing noises; certain someone was trying to break in."

"That's normal," Gloria said. She didn't mention that Margaret had not returned her call.

The important thing was she was there and she was okay, at least physically. The emotional healing would take months or even years, if ever.

Gloria led the way into the kitchen and the group surrounded Margaret as they hugged her and offered words of encouragement and support.

Margaret put on a brave face as she thanked them for their concern and assured them she would be all right.

The breakfast bake had just finished baking and Gloria pulled it from the oven. She set it on the kitchen counter, next to the donuts, pastries, bagels and large pan of bacon, sausage and ham Dot had brought.

Andrea and Alice were the last to arrive and Alice placed the large glass dish of the Spanish bread pudding alongside the rest of the food.

Gloria uncovered the dish and the smell of cinnamon wafted up. "It looks and smells delicious," she told Alice as she placed the cover on top of the microwave.

Since the large group wouldn't all be able to fit around the kitchen table, Gloria had dragged a couple card tables and folding chairs from the attic and lined them up in the center of the kitchen.

After everyone was seated, Gloria spoke. "Thank you all for coming here on such short notice." She smiled at Margaret. "Thank you, Margaret, for coming. We know this is a difficult time for you and we want to be here for you."

"Day or night," Ruth piped up.

"We're only a phone call away," Lucy said.

"And if you won't call us, we'll call you," Andrea said.

"Let's pray." The women bowed their heads and Gloria began to pray. "Thank you Heavenly Father, for bringing us all together this morning.

Thank you for this wonderful food we're about to enjoy."

"Lord, we lift up Margaret to you this morning. You know what a difficult time she's been going through, that her heart is heavy as she mourns the loss of her husband. Lord, we ask that you comfort her with your presence in the days and months ahead. We ask that you help her physically, emotionally and financially as she begins this next chapter in her life. We thank you, Lord for your gift of salvation, that we're always mindful of our many blessings, in Jesus name."

"Amen." They all said in unison.

Margaret dabbed at her eyes. "Thank you," she whispered. "That was beautiful." She eyed the plentiful dishes of food on the counter. "I'm not very hungry."

"Try to eat something. You might surprise yourself." Gloria led her to the end of the counter and handed her a plate.

She turned to the others, still seated. "Don't be shy." She waved her hands. "Get it while it's hot."

Gloria waited until the others had filled their plates before filling her own.

"This is your seat." Rose patted the empty chair next to her, on the other side of Margaret. The women oohed and aahed over the breakfast bake, the Spanish bread not to mention the other goodies Dot and Rose had brought with them.

Margaret finished her breakfast first and she stared at her empty plate in disbelief. "I can't believe I ate all my food."

"There's more where that came from."

"No. I'm full." Margaret patted her stomach. "I think I'll have a little more coffee. The cinnamon dish was delicious. All of it was delicious." She refilled her cup and returned to her seat.

“How is the investigation going?” Gloria had gone back and forth as to whether she should bring up Don’s death but decided it wasn’t far from anyone’s mind, including Margaret’s.

Margaret rubbed her forehead. “Oh. I forgot to tell you. Detective Givens said they are ruling Don’s death accidental.”

“So they’ve dropped the investigation,” Ruth said.

“Yes. Lack of evidence, inconclusive, whatever. I think the detective felt sorry for me. With everything that happened, I forgot Don had taken out a life insurance policy years ago. It was for a substantial amount. I contacted the company yesterday and they’re processing the claim.”

“If the authorities had ruled Don’s death a suicide, you might not have been able to collect,” Andrea said. “It depends on the age of the policy.” Andrea’s first husband, Daniel Malone, had owned an insurance agency and she was familiar with many of the stipulations and rules of standard policies.

"The policy was almost ten years old so even if they'd ruled his death a suicide, the claim was still valid." Margaret sipped her coffee. "I still can't accept the fact Don took the money from all of those retirement accounts, not to mention our bank and savings account. How could he have done such a thing?"

"Maybe he planned to invest the money, hoping to accumulate even more." Gloria thought of the Ponzi scheme the men at the golf club had mentioned. "Did he mention investing in a business venture recently?"

"No." Margaret shook her head. "Not a peep, other than what George at the bank told Chad and me. You were going to visit the country club yesterday. Any success?"

Liz cleared her throat. "Yeah. We've got a few leads. We were wondering if you could give us a list of close friends Don golfed with so we could do a little intel."

"That and if he had a pattern of when he played golf," Gloria added.

"Of course. I'm sorry. I know you asked who he golfed with the other day." Margaret lifted her hand and waved it over her head. "Everything has gone over my head. I'm lucky if I remember what day it is."

She continued. "Don had a 1:00 standing tee time every Saturday and played with a small group of buddies he regularly golfed and hung out with. Club NED."

"Club NED?" Dot asked.

"Yeah. Club NED was their nickname around the country club for always playing together and hanging out afterward. There was Nolan Bolton, Ed Shields, Don of course and the fourth player changed but was usually one of the co-owners, Phil Holt."

"What about a woman...Becky something?" Liz asked.

Margaret frowned. "Becky." She shook her head. "No. I don't know anyone named Becky. Where did you come up with that name?"

"We were looking at Montbay Hills' social media site and found a picture of Don standing with two other men and a woman and it listed her as Becky something," Gloria said. "We should go over there later today, play a little golf. If the others kept the tee time, we might get lucky and run into Don's golf partners. Club NED."

Gloria didn't mention the Ponzi scheme. She wanted to throw some bait out there since at this point it was merely speculation.

"Today just happens to be Saturday," Gloria said. "Who's up for a few rounds of golf with Liz and me?"

Lucy's hand shot up.

Rose shook her head. "No way."

"I'm afraid I'm out," Dot said.

"I've got to work or I would go," Ruth said.

"I've shot a few rounds," Andrea said. "I could be the fourth player."

Gloria pointed around the room. "Lucy, Andrea, Liz and me. Let's leave here around 12:30 and see if we can do a little recon on Don's buddies."

"Don't forget there's a golf tournament tomorrow with a large party at the clubhouse," Liz said.

"You're right," Margaret said. "I forgot all about it. Everyone who is anyone at the country club will be there."

"Are you going to the party?" Margaret asked. "It's by member invite only and technically you're not members. I could extend an invitation since I'm still a member."

"We met some guys in the Snack Shack near the back of the course. We started a conversation and one of them invited us to the party," Liz said.

"Liz was pouring on the charm," Gloria joked. "We didn't get a last name but his first name was Rex. She's already forgotten about her gigolo boyfriend."

"Martin is not a gigolo," Liz insisted. "You'll see, just as soon as we're able to track him down."

"Martin?" Lucy turned in her chair to face Liz. "Gigolo? What have I missed?"

Gloria briefly explained Liz's dilemma and told the group Liz had asked her to track down her boyfriend and the money. "She thinks he's in Poughkeepsie, New York."

"If he's a golf pro, he's probably on NGPD." Margaret explained *NGPD*, or National Golf Pro Directory was a database that kept track of all of the golf pros in the United States. "Don was looking for one of the old golf pros he met years ago when we first joined the country club and Phil, one of the owners, showed him the system. He was able to track the man down in California."

Liz's eyes lit. "Montbay Hills has access to this database?"

Gloria could see the wheels spinning in Liz's head. "Oh no..."

"Oh yes!" Liz screeched. "I'm gonna track down Martin Heemingstar if it's the last thing I do!"

# Chapter 17

Gloria spotted the car Margaret had described as soon as she drove into the country club. "That looks like it could be Ed Shields' Silver Lincoln MKZ." She pulled into the parking spot next to it, reached for the door handle and turned to her friends. "Remember, we're a group of wealthy women who're looking to invest in something where we can make some quick cash."

"Yep." Lucy gave two thumbs up. "We have money to invest and we're looking to get rich quick."

Liz had already set thc tee time for 1:10 p.m., hoping they would run into Don's former golf partners either in the clubhouse or on the green. It looked like their gamble might actually pay off.

The women strode across the parking lot. "We should use Andrea as our lead in. Those men will swoon all over her," Liz said.

Gloria had to agree. Andrea, who had had a country club membership when her first husband, Daniel, was alive, was dressed to impress in a pastel print skirt she explained was a *skort*. Her matching pink polo blouse and bright yellow visor completed the ensemble.

Gloria eyed the color-coordinated outfit. "I should shop with you more." She glanced at her own drab gray Capri slacks, short sleeve button down blouse and dull black visor she'd borrowed from Paul.

"You look fine," Lucy said. "This isn't a fashion contest."

"True."

The women waited outside while Liz headed inside to get the key to the cart and a set of rental clubs. Andrea brought her own clubs and offered to share so they would only have to borrow one set of clubs.

Gloria glanced at her watch. “What is taking Liz so long?” She started to follow her sister into the building when Liz popped out, dangling the golf cart key. “I managed to find out Don’s former golfing buddies are already on the green. They’ve got about a ten minute head start on us.”

The women hurried to the golf cart, parked next to the building and climbed in. Andrea and Liz sat in the front while Lucy and Gloria settled onto the bench seat. “We can hurry through the first hole and hopefully catch them on the second or third.”

Liz stomped on the gas and Gloria gripped the side of the cart. “Easy Liz. This isn’t a race cart.” Liz ignored her sister as she zipped along the winding path to the first hole. She came to an abrupt halt and hopped out.

“You go first.” Liz told Andrea.

"10-4." Andrea saluted Liz and hurried to the first tee.

Although Gloria knew next to nothing about golf, she could see Andrea was a natural as she eyed the ball and the flag before pulling her club back and effortlessly hitting the ball.

"Nice shot," Liz said. She turned to Lucy. "You said it's been years since you golfed with your old beau, Ben. You might want to take notes."

"Bill," Lucy said. "His name was Bill."

Gloria leaned on her golf club. "I wonder if he's still doing time."

"I hope so," Lucy said. "What a jerk. How I ever got involved with that man, I'll never know."

"Don't be too hard on yourself," Gloria said. "Look at how many questionable choices Liz has made in men."

Liz shot her sister a death look. "So I made one bad judgment of character."

"One?" Gloria laughed. "Not counting the traveling salesman who talked you into accompanying him to Florida where he took all your money and you called me and begged me to send you some cash for the bus fare home." She tapped the golf club on the green. "Now that I think about it, maybe you should move back to Michigan. You don't have much luck with Florida men."

Liz ignored her sister's jabs as she studied the ball she'd placed on the tee. "Watch and learn." She swung at the ball and hit it first try.

"Nice shot. I guess I'll give it a whack." Lucy set her ball on the tee and took a swing. She missed the first and second try.

"Focus," Liz said. "You need to focus."

"I'm better at firing weapons, not swinging them." Lucy studied the ball, lifted her club and swung, making contact with the ball on her third attempt. "Third time is the charm."

Gloria was next and she was able to send the ball flying on her second attempt.

"Pick it up gals." Liz darted across the meticulously manicured green and hurried to the cart. Gloria was barely on the bench seat when Liz sped off down the path.

They hurried to finish the first hole and unanimously decided to skip the second hole in an attempt to catch up with Ed Shields and the others.

"I think we found Club NED." Gloria pointed at a golf cart. It crested a small hill and disappeared over the other side.

"Hang on ladies." Liz stomped on the foot pedal. The cart picked up speed as it careened off the paved path and climbed the hill.

They crested the hill and Gloria squeezed her eyes shut when she realized the other golf cart had stopped on top of the hill.

Liz stomped on the brake and jerked the wheel in an attempt to avoid a cart collision.

"Liz," Gloria gasped.

"Sorry."

The golfers, who stood next to the tee, spun around when they caught a glimpse of the speeding cart coming toward them.

"Watch where you're going!" one of the men shouted. "You almost hit our cart."

"Maybe you shouldn't park on the top of a hill!" Liz shot back.

Andrea sprang from her seat and hurried toward the tee. "I'm so sorry. We're new and the course is unfamiliar to us."

"I'm a guest." Andrea pointed at Gloria. "She's a new member."

"Not for long at this rate," Gloria mumbled under her breath.

"Ah." One of the men rested his hands lightly on top of his golf club. "Kind of late in the season to take up golfing, isn't it?"

"I live in Florida and can golf year-round," Liz answered haughtily, still put off by the gruff reprimand of her driving skills. "Ever heard of Royal Palms Plantation Country Club in Windermere?"

The man lifted a brow. "Yeah. Royal Palms is a championship golf course. I've played there a time or two. You live in Windermere?"

"Close," Liz said.

"If you have such a great golf club down there, why are you playing at Montbay Hills?"

"I'm here visiting my sister, Gloria." Liz pointed to her sister. "I'm in town trying to help her set up some local investments."

Gloria hurried forward. "I'm trying to leverage some money."

"She needs to make some quick cash," Liz said bluntly. "I've got a small amount of expertise in that area and am here to try to help."

Gloria choked on Liz's words and her sister shot her a dirty look.

"Interesting. I might be able to assist you." One of the other men stepped forward and held out his hand. "I'm Ed Shields, sales trader by day. I also help friends secure killer investments."

"What's a sales trader?" Gloria had never heard the phrase.

"In a nutshell, I represent institutional accounts in the equity marketplace by serving as the communication conduit between clients and equity traders. I also provide clients with research, trading suggestions and capital commitment, acting as the "eyes and ears" of my clients in the equity marketplace by identifying trends in the marketplace and providing market color to clients."

The lengthy explanation went right over Gloria's head and it sounded like a bunch of mumbo jumbo.

"In other words, you help your clients make money," Andrea said.

"Exactly." Ed smiled at Andrea. "Perhaps fate brought you here. I think I...we...might be able to help."

Another man in Ed's party stepped forward. "You know the rules...no shop talk on the greens."

"True." Ed smiled a toothy white grin. "Perhaps we can meet in the clubhouse for a drink after we finish?"

"Yes. I mean maybe." Gloria didn't want to appear too eager.

"Of course," Liz said. "We'll meet you in the clubhouse." They waited for the foursome to move onto the next hole before speaking.

“We need to dig into this a little deeper,” Lucy said. “I say we see what he has to say.”

“Agreed. I just didn’t want to seem too eager,” Gloria said.

“Remember, you’re desperate to make money,” Lucy reminded her.

“Good point.” The women played the next hole. They gave up after playing fourteen holes and made a unanimous decision to head to the clubhouse in an attempt to talk to some of the other members.

Liz returned the cart while Andrea, Lucy and Gloria headed to the club’s lounge. The day had become overcast and it added to the gloom of the darkly paneled room. The lingering smell of stale cigarette smokc filled the air.

There was a sign next to the entrance. ‘*Open to the public.*’

The room was virtually empty, except for the bartender and a couple of men who were sitting at the bar watching a golf game on the television.

"Go where the action is," Andrea joked in a whispered voice.

The trio headed to the bar area and settled in not far from the men.

The bartender meandered over. "What can I get you lovely ladies?"

"What kind of iced tea do you have?" Gloria asked.

"Raspberry, Blackberry, Mint Julep, Sweet and unsweet," he said.

"Raspberry sounds good," Gloria said.

"Make it two," Andrea said.

"I'll make it easy," Lucy said. "Make it three."

Liz wandered in as the bartender placed the drinks in front of the women. She hopped onto an empty barstool. "Whatcha having?"

"Tea." Gloria swirled the ice cubes with her straw and sipped.

"Perfect," Liz said. "Make mine a Long Island."

"Liz," Gloria said.

"What? Make it a double," she told the bartender. "I'm not driving."

Her sister's eyes narrowed.

"Okay. Make it a single." She tilted her head and gazed at the men sitting at the other end of the bar.

Gloria shook her head. "We haven't talked to them yet."

The bartender returned moments later, placed a paper napkin on the bar and the mixed drink on top.

Liz sipped the drink. "Perfect." She grabbed the napkin and hopped off the barstool. "Watch and learn."

# Chapter 18

"Mind if I sit here?" Liz didn't wait for an answer as she hopped onto the barstool and set her drink on top of the bar. "You fellas members here?"

The man closest to Liz nodded. "Yeah. You?"

"Just visiting," Liz replied. "We're waiting for someone. Ed Shields."

The man grabbed his drink and sipped. "Club NED."

"I heard the nickname before. What does it mean?"

"They're a group of bigshot shysters." The man next to him blurted out.

"Crooks?" Gloria wandered over and stood behind Liz.

As if on cue, Ed Shields and his golfing partners entered the pub and headed their way.

"They prey on newbies," the second man said in a low voice. "I gotta go." He slid off the barstool and quickly exited the bar, passing Ed and his group of friends on his way out.

"Afternoon Gus." Ed nodded at the lone man seated at the bar.

He turned to Liz and the other women. "Let's have a seat at a corner table where it's quiet and we can talk."

The women followed Ed and the others to the far side of the room, to a table situated in front of the large picture windows that overlooked the golf course.

Gloria pulled out a chair and sat. "How does your investment program work?"

"What's the minimum?" Liz asked.

"The minimum is ten thousand but we prefer twenty. That's when you really start seeing a significant return," Ed said.

"How long before we start seeing a return?"

"Within 30 days, guaranteed 30% ROI...return on investment...or your money back."

Gloria lifted a brow. "That's impressive."

Nolan Bolton leaned forward. "These gentleman use the money for a variety of investments, mostly unsecured, but rest assured they personally screen each one and as partners unanimously agree on the venture."

"Who are the partners if you don't mind me asking," Lucy said.

"Actually, we do mind." A man who hadn't introduced himself yet but Gloria recognized him from the internet photo as Phil Holt, one of the co-owners of the golf club. "They are silent partners by choice." He leaned back in his chair and crossed his arms. "If you don't trust us, then don't invest."

Gloria lifted a hand. "No need to be defensive. I believe it was a legitimate question."

"The main contacts are us." Ed nodded to his colleagues. "We can provide you with financials from last year if you like."

"Yes, I would like to see them," Gloria said. "We plan to attend the after tournament party tomorrow evening. If you could email a copy of the financials and everything looks acceptable, I'll bring a money order/cashier's check with me tomorrow." She wanted to get her hands on the financials to see if she could glean any information on the scammers.

"If Gloria is happy with her investment, I might look into investing as well," Andrea said.

Ed rubbed his hands together. The look of glee on his face made Gloria want to laugh. She was certain the word *sucker* was running through his head. It was like a cat and mouse game. She wondered how Don had ever gotten involved in such a racket.

Ed plucked his cell phone from his jacket pocket. "Give me your email address and we'll have the financials sent over within the hour."

Gloria rattled off her email address and stood. She turned to a woman who had wandered over during the conversation and who so far had remained silent. "I'm sorry. I didn't catch your name."

The woman smiled. "Becky."

"Becky?" Gloria already knew her last name was Stone but wondered if she would tell her and if not, why she was keeping it a secret.

"Just Becky," she said.

"Are you a partner, too?" Lucy asked.

"In a roundabout way," Becky replied.

Phil Holt stood, a sign the meeting had ended. "I need to take care of some paperwork in my office." He turned to Gloria. "It was a pleasure meeting you lovely ladies. Are all of you attending the party tomorrow night?"

"I'm not sure," Gloria said.

"It's invitation only," Phil said.

"Yes. We met..." Gloria couldn't remember the man's name who'd invited them.

"Rex invited us," Liz said. "We met him the other day at the Snack Shack.

"Rex Wetzel." Phil gave Ed a quick glance. "I'll see you ladies hopefully tomorrow evening then."

Phil exited the pub.

Gloria waited until he was out of sight. "We should be leaving, as well."

Ed and Nolan stood.

Becky remained seated.

"It was a pleasure meeting you." Ed shook Gloria's hand. "I hope we can do business and make you an even wealthier woman."

“Your venture sounds intriguing,” Gloria said. “I can’t wait to take a look at the financials and discuss it with my friends.” She almost said ‘my husband’ but didn’t want them to know she was married. If the men and Becky found out she was married to a retired cop, it would throw off their sting.

They parted ways on the sidewalk out front and the women walked to the car.

“What do you think?” Andrea asked.

“I smell a rat,” Liz said.

“Don was a bank vice president for many years,” Lucy said. “How could he possibly have become caught up in a Ponzi scheme? I mean, he would be savvy to stuff like that.”

“Greed,” Andrea said. “I’m not saying this was the case, but greed can blind you to a lot of things.”

“Including common sense,” Gloria said. “What happens if we show up tomorrow, I don’t have the cash on hand and these four call my bluff?"

"We'll think of something," Liz said. "Maybe you can tell them the money is tied up in CDs and you've got to wait for the paperwork to process before you can take it out."

"Or tell them you're still thinking about it. You want to mull it over for a couple days," Andrea said.

"Yeah." Gloria nodded. "That's what I'll do...tell them I need a couple more days to think about it."

Gloria dropped Andrea off at home first and then Lucy, before she and Liz headed to the farm. It was late afternoon and Paul was still at the museum. It had been a long golf game and she was stiff from the physical exertion, not to mention the tennis game from the previous day.

Liz headed to her room while Gloria and Mally made their way outside. There was still several hours of daylight left and she decided it would be a good time to take a walk through the gardens and flowerbeds. Mally trotted ahead and then circled back as if to tell Gloria to hurry up.

The fresh air helped clear her head and she wondered once again if Don's death was a suicide, or perhaps it was an accident. Perhaps he hadn't meant to kill himself. There was still the possibility someone had murdered him and attempted to make it look like a suicide, although the police had officially called it accidental.

A shiver ran down her spine at the thought. If there were a killer running around, would he or she suspect Margaret knew something and they planned to take her out, as well?

Perhaps Don had been taken in the Ponzi scheme and when he threatened to expose the schemers, they murdered him.

From the brief interaction with Don's former golf partners, Gloria guessed Ed Shields was the speaker of the group. Nolan Bolton was right behind him. The other two, Phil Holt and Becky

Stone, seemed more subdued. Perhaps they were the leaders and the other two the recruiters.

Rex Wetzel knew something. She remembered the comment he'd made, alluding to the schemers. Maybe he was part of it, too. Maybe he was a "recruiter." She made a mental note to have Liz cozy up to him at the party since he seemed to have taken a liking to her.

By the time Gloria circled the barn, Paul was pulling in the drive. He'd called to tell her not to fix dinner and had stopped to pick up some food on his way.

While they walked to the house, she reminded him she wouldn't be home Sunday evening because Liz and she planned to attend the tournament's evening party and then she told him what they'd discovered earlier in the day.

"You don't plan on giving these clowns any money, do you?" Paul asked.

"No. We're going to put them off, which reminds me, they promised to email me a copy of the profit and loss statement."

After dinner, Gloria hurried to the computer. The email was in her inbox and Liz pulled up a chair so the women could pore over the papers together.

At first glance, the companies looked legit but Gloria wasn't convinced. She printed off the statement so they could do some research. Several were legitimate companies and she was beginning to wonder if they were on a wild goose chase.

It wasn't until she got to the bottom of the list, her radar went up. Gloria waved the paper at Liz. "Check this one out. This company's website claims they're a luxury resort on some remote island I've never heard of. Pelletree."

They found a couple more that raised red flags and Gloria highlighted them so she could dig a little deeper into their backgrounds.

Paul wandered into the dining room. "You 'bout ready for bed? I have a full day at the museum and we gotta get up early."

"Yeah." Gloria pushed her chair back. "We may be onto something."

"Just be careful," Paul warned. "You don't know if these people are dangerous. If they're running an illegal scheme and they think you're onto them, you could all be in danger."

"I'll have Lucy go with us. She'll be packing heat," Gloria said.

Paul rolled his eyes. "Great. Now I am concerned."

"Don't worry." Gloria hugged her husband. "I've got it all under control."

# Chapter 19

"Let's go over the plan one more time," Gloria said. "Ruth, you and Dot are going to stay inside Ruth's van for audio and visual surveillance."

"Andrea, Lucy, Liz and I are going to go inside and mingle with the club members and also mention to them we're considering investing with Club NED members to see if any of them react."

"I'm going to track down Rex Wetzel and hopefully figure out if he's involved with the investment group," Liz added.

"Lucy is going to stick close to me in case Ed or Nolan start acting weird when I question them about some of the investment prospects and tell them I need to think about it over the weekend."

Lucy patted her pocket. "We may have a problem if the club's security is checking each of the party attendees with those handheld weapon wands."

"You brought a weapon?" Dot stared at Lucy's pocket.

"Are you surprised?" Andrea asked.

"No, I guess not."

"I'm carrying it legally," Lucy said. "And I don't intend to fire it unless absolutely necessary."

Visions of Lucy brandishing her weapon and people stampeding out of the clubhouse filled Gloria's head. "It's probably a good thing I only have a month membership. Tonight might be the end of it if things get out of hand."

"They won't," Lucy said confidently. "I know how to handle tight situations."

"Like the one in Nantucket where Barnacle Bill was shooting at you?" Gloria teased.

"It wasn't my fault," Lucy argued. "The man was crazy."

Ruth drove into the parking lot and circled it once before deciding on the perfect stakeout location. She backed into the spot and shifted to park. "This spot is perfect. I can keep one surveillance camera pointed at the front door and another on the entrance to the parking lot."

"You can't watch both at once," Liz said.

"I can't." Ruth pointed at her eyes. "That's why Dot is here. She has a sharp eye."

"Thanks Ruth." Dot beamed. "I didn't think I had a useful skill."

"Don't sell yourself short," Ruth said. "You're a perfect partner in non-crime."

Gloria reached for the side door handle. "Remember, no matter what you do or what you see...*do not engage*."

"Pfft." Ruth waved her hand. "This ain't our first rodeo."

“I know but a reminder never hurts.” Gloria glanced at Lucy. “It’s time to roll.”

Despite the modest wedge heels Gloria was wearing, she teetered when she stepped onto the asphalt. Lucy was next. Liz piled out after her and Andrea brought up the rear.

Gloria eyed Andrea’s shimmering party dress. “Wow. You look smokin’ hot. Brian let you out of the house dressed like that?” she joked.

Andrea tugged on the beaded collar. “Yeah. Does it make me look like a hoochie?”

“Not at all. You look classy,” Gloria said.

“Yeah. You’ll be a useful distraction,” Liz said. “The outfit is perfect.”

The girls joined the small group of guests waiting in line to get inside. Country club personnel stood guard at the door, checking the guests’ names against a clipboard list.

“I hope Rex didn’t forget to add your name,” Gloria whispered.

"Don't worry. Even if he did, I'm going to get us in there," Liz promised.

"Great. It makes me feel so much better. Not."

They reached the front of the line.

"Name please?"

"Liz Applegate."

The man, pen in hand, scanned the list. "I don't..."

Gloria's stomach knotted. Visions of Liz creating a scene flashed through her mind.

"Uh. There you are." The man checked her name off the list. "These are your friends?"

"Yes." Liz nodded and the man waved the women through.

"Whew! That was close," Lucy said as she patted her pocket.

The soft strains of a piano filled the reception area. Uniformed butlers carried trays of champagne flutes as they offered them to the new arrivals.

"No thanks." Gloria shook her head as one stopped by to offer a drink. "Let's head into the main reception room." She led the way and the women crossed the entry, passed through a large set of double doors and entered an enormous reception room.

Large tables filled the four corners of the crowded room. Liquor bottles filled one of the tables. A second table was loaded with hors d' oeuvres, the third light entrees and the fourth was a decadent dessert table.

"We might as well indulge in the goodies." Liz made a beeline for the array of bite size appetizers.

"She's right," Lucy said. "I don't know if I've ever been to such a hoity-toity event."

The women trailed behind Liz and Gloria stood off to the side as she perused the offerings. She wasn't a fan of sushi or food she couldn't identify. "What is that?" She pointed to a small round piece of red meat. In the center was what appeared to be raw egg yolk.

The woman behind the table placed her hands behind her back. "Steak tartare."

"Steak tartare?"

"Raw red beef with an egg yolk in the center," she replied. "Would you care to try it?"

Gloria made a gagging sound and Lucy snorted. "That would be a big *no*."

There were several other unidentifiable offerings and Gloria finally settled on a piece of crusty bread with a red sauce and melted cheese. She nibbled the edge as she cased the joint. "I don't see any of the Club NED peeps yet."

"Liz found Rex." Andrea tilted her head to the side. "Hopefully she's thanking him for the invite."

Liz snaked her arm through Rex's and leaned close to whisper in his ear.

Gloria popped the rest of the tasty morsel in her mouth. "Yeah. She's thanking him all right."

After Gloria finished her appetizer, they strolled over to the entrée table and she let out the breath she'd been holding when she recognized cooked meatballs floating in brown gravy, petite sausage links, a platter of flaky dinner rolls, bowls of pasta with cream sauce and a tray of seasoned asparagus. "This is more like it." She sampled one of the pasta dishes, a spear of asparagus, a couple meatballs and a dinner roll.

"I wonder if they would be willing to give me the asparagus recipe," she whispered to Andrea, who joined her near the end of the table. "Mine always turns out mushy and under seasoned."

Lucy quickly finished her entrée and made a beeline for the decadent dessert table. "I'm surprised it took this long for Lucy to hit the sweet stuff," Gloria said. "I figured she would have headed there first."

Lucy loaded two plates and wandered over. "Check these out." Lucy held out her dishes, crammed full of sweet treats. "There's a cheesecake-swirl brownie, carrot cake, red velvet cake. They even have baklava." She balanced both plates, reached for the layered sugar-filled pastry and nibbled the edge. "This is delicious!"

Gloria had tried baklava once and it was too sugary for her tastes, which meant it was probably perfect for her best friend. She snaked past Lucy. "Where did Liz go?" She caught a glimpse of Rex, mingling with other guests. Liz was nowhere in sight.

Lucy shrugged. "Hard telling with Liz."

"Hello ladies." Gloria jumped at the deep voice behind her and spun around. It was Ed Shields and he was alone.

"Hello Mr. Shields."

"All my friends call me Ed," he said. "I trust you got the information we forwarded yesterday?"

"I did." Gloria nodded. "I'm still reviewing it, although I do have some questions."

"So you still haven't reached a decision?" he asked.

"N-not yet," Gloria stammered. "I decided to give myself the weekend to mull it over. Twenty thousand is a lot of money to just hand over."

"I'm thinking of investing, too," Andrea chimed in. "Unless, of course, you're not looking for more investors?"

"We are." Ed Shields smiled, his gleaming white teeth filling his face. "We're always looking for solid investment partners. Perhaps we can have lunch Tuesday?"

"Perhaps." Gloria quickly changed the subject. "What a lovely party turnout. I think someone mentioned Mr. Holt was one of the owners. Are there many more?"

"There are three partners who jointly own Montbay Hills Golf & Country Club. Mr. Holt,

Dylan Nestor. He's a silent partner who lives out in California and then there's Becky Stone. I believe she was golfing with us the other day when we met."

Warning bells rang in Gloria's head. When she had questioned Margaret about Becky Stone, Margaret claimed she didn't even know who the woman was. As a long-standing member, surely Margaret knew who owned the golf club!

"I see. It sounds like a well-rounded group and I like the fact that the golf club is equal opportunity."

A butler approached and tapped Ed on the shoulder. "If you'll excuse me." He spun on his heel and then wove his way through the crowd to the other side of the room.

"Did you hear that?" Andrea whispered. "He said the woman is a co-owner and Margaret had no idea who she was."

The list of potential schemers was growing. Not only was Rex Wetzel on the radar, so was Ed

Shields, Phil Holt, Nolan Bolton and Becky Stone. Perhaps they were dealing with a larger ring of scam artists than Gloria originally thought. What if one of them was not only a scam artist, but also a killer?

Lucy hurried toward them. “I’ve looked everywhere for Liz, including the women’s restroom. She’s gone.”

# Chapter 20

"Is she in Ruth's van?" Gloria asked.

"Nope." Lucy shook her head. "I already checked."

"Let's spread out. Andrea, you take the appetizer and drinks side. Lucy, you take the entrée and dessert side. I'll search the front reception area and the restrooms again. We'll meet up outside the main doors."

The women split up as they searched for Liz. Lucy was right. Liz had vanished.

Gloria met the women out front a short time later. "The last time I saw her, she was talking to Rex Wetzel."

"Try her cell phone," Andrea suggested.

"Good idea." Gloria pulled her cell phone from her purse and dialed Liz's cell phone. It went directly to voice mail. "Liz. We're here at the party and can't find you. Please call me as soon as you get this message."

She dropped the cell phone inside her purse and gazed around. The sun had set and it was starting to get dark. Gloria's eyes fell on Ruth's van, parked near a street light and she hurried across the parking lot.

Ruth opened the side door. "Still no Liz?"

"No," Gloria said. "I'm getting worried. You didn't happen to see her come out?"

"Nope." Ruth shook her head.

"We haven't taken our eyes off the entrance to this place or the front doors," Dot confirmed.

"We haven't searched outside," Lucy said.

"True. Let's circle the building. I saw a large terraced patio out back. Maybe she went out there with someone."

Gloria, Andrea and Lucy headed to the side of the building and Ruth promised to call Gloria's cell if she was able to get a visual on Liz.

"When I find her, I'm going to strangle her," Gloria vowed. "She knows better than to run off without telling us where she's going."

"Maybe she wasn't thinking." Andrea picked up the pace to keep up with Gloria.

"I'm sure she's fine," Lucy said. "You know how she is when she gets something in her head and acts impulsively."

"That's what I'm worried about." Gloria stepped off the sidewalk and passed the pro shop where she noticed the lights were on. She didn't slow her pace as she glanced in the windows.

She had almost passed by the window when she caught a glimpse of Liz's blonde head. She was behind the cashier's counter, peering at a computer screen.

"Liz," Gloria gasped. "She's in the store."

Gloria retraced her steps to the store door and grabbed the knob. The door was locked so she tapped on the window.

Liz glanced up, a deer in the headlights look on her face. She held up a finger and turned her attention to the man standing next to her.

Andrea eased in next to Gloria and peered into the store. "I hope she's onto something good."

A few moments later, Liz hurried to the door and opened it. "What are you doing here?"

"I might ask you the same thing," Gloria hissed. "We've been tearing this place apart, looking for you."

"We thought something happened to you," Lucy added.

"I'm fine. I'm just taking a short break from the party," Liz said. "Ivan, one of the golf pros, was just showing me a few things. I'll be back inside in a minute."

Gloria opened her mouth to say something but before she could speak, Liz shut the door in her face. They heard the lock click.

"She makes me so mad!" Gloria clenched her fists. "I have half a mind to leave her here and let her find her own way home."

"What if she's onto something?" Andrea asked. "We should give her the benefit of the doubt."

Gloria turned on her heel and stomped down the sidewalk. "Maybe she's looking for Martin. I hope she finds him."

"I'm going to grab a couple more goodies," Lucy said when they reached the reception room. "I want to try one of the chocolate cupcakes."

"Wait!" Gloria grabbed her arm. "Check it out. Over by the fireplace." Becky Stone and Phil Holt hovered near the fireplace. They were talking to Rex Wetzel and none other than Ed Shields.

Gloria turned so her back was to them.

"Ah." Lucy narrowed her eyes. "Judging by the serious expressions, they're having a very important conversation."

Liz returned a short time later and when Gloria tried to question her sister about what she was doing, she was vague. "Ivan was kind enough to show me the ins and outs of their database. It was all very fascinating."

"Were you able to track down lover boy?" Gloria asked.

"Maybe." Liz shrugged. "I had an interesting conversation with Rex Wetzel earlier. I think he's in on the scheme. He told me he had the inside scoop on how I could make substantial sums of money."

"When I pointed out the other day he said something about a money scheme, he told me he was only joking but I think he was lying."

Liz studied her nails. "I broke a nail trying to type on the keyboard." She lowered her hand. "Anyhoo, I'm meeting Rex for lunch tomorrow.

He said he could hook me up with some great investments and outright warned me to steer clear of Ed Shields and the others. He seems like a sincere guy but I still get an uneasy feeling he might be trying to pull one over on me."

"You're such a great judge of character, Liz. I'd be shocked anyone could pull one over on you," Gloria said with a hint of sarcasm.

"Dig all you want. At least I'm onto something," Liz sniffed. "What have you come up with?"

"We found out Becky Stone, the woman Margaret had no idea who she was, is one of the co-owners of this joint."

Liz's eyes widened. "Really?" She shifted to the side and glanced at the group, still standing in front of the fireplace. "What if the owners are in on the money making scheme? Think about it. This is a prestigious golf club. Many of the members have big bucks. What a perfect place to find suckers."

"I think you're right," Lucy said. "Ed Shields wants to meet Gloria Tuesday. If you can't find anything out from Rex when you have lunch with him tomorrow, we might have to move onto Plan B."

Gloria started to shake her head. "I don't think Paul will be keen on the idea of me meeting a man alone. I'm not sure *I* like the idea of meeting that man, or any man, alone."

"Don't worry," Andrea said. "I'll come with you. After all, you want your daughter to help you make sound financial decisions."

"Andrea, you're an angel," Gloria said. "We'll see what Liz manages to find out tomorrow and go from there. I have Ed's contact information from the questionable financials. I can call him tomorrow night."

The women stayed for another half an hour and mingled with several of the guests as Gloria introduced herself as a potential new member. Despite dropping several hints about looking for investments, none of them mentioned Ed Shields or his "investment opportunities."

By eight o'clock, Gloria had had enough. "Let's wrap this up."

"I agree." Andrea yawned and covered her mouth. "Brian just texted to ask me when I was coming home."

"I'm sorry Andrea. I keep forgetting you're still newlyweds," Gloria said.

"Semi-newlyweds," Andrea said. "He's fine. He just worries about me."

"He knows I'll keep you out of trouble," Gloria said.

Andrea laughed. "Right. That's exactly what he's worried about...you all getting me into trouble."

The four women walked toward the exit. "He knew what he was getting into when he married you."

“Yes, he did.” Andrea put her arm around Gloria’s shoulder. “Don’t worry Mom. He’ll be fine.”

When they reached Ruth’s van, Gloria let the others in first and then climbed inside. She turned to Ruth. “Well? Did you get anything good?”

Ruth crawled across the floor to the driver’s seat and started the van. “We got a few shots of the men in question. Several cigarette smokers came out to light up. We also noticed several groups of guests milling about outside.”

“Ruth turned her audio on but there was too much white noise to hear what they were saying, although you could tell from the look on their faces they were having serious conversations,” Dot said.

“We saw a definite pattern.” Ruth shifted into drive and pulled out of the parking spot. “There seemed to be a ringleader. The same person came out every single time.”

"Any mention of names?" Gloria asked.

"No, but we have the footage," Ruth said. "Show 'em what we got."

Dot leaned over the panel of screens on the sidewall and flipped a switch. A grainy image popped up on the screen. "It'll take me a sec to zoom in."

The image cleared and Rex Wetzel's face appeared. "This guy came out almost every single time but with different people." Dot shifted in her seat.

"Every ten minutes," Ruth said. "We timed it."

"That's Rex Wetzel," Liz said. "He must be the ringleader."

Gloria told the others Liz was meeting Rex for lunch the following day. "You'll need to be very careful Liz."

"I will," Liz said. "We're meeting at some taco place called *North of the Border* in Green Springs."

"Oh! I've been dying to try *North of the Border*," Andrea said. "Maybe I can talk Brian and Alice into going so we can keep an eye on you."

"Rex has seen your face," Gloria pointed out.

"True." Andrea looked crestfallen.

"I would go but he's met Lucy and me, too."

"I've got to work tomorrow," Dot said.

They all turned to Ruth. "I love Mexican food. I can take an extended lunch. Maybe Alice will go with me."

"Or Rose," Dot said.

Ruth agreed to dine at the restaurant at the same time Liz planned to meet Rex.

Earlier, the group had met in front of Dot's Restaurant where they'd parked their cars so they could ride together in Ruth's van.

Gloria waited for the others to exit the van. She was the last one out. "Thanks for the backup, Ruth. I gotta tell you, when I first found out about all this spy stuff you installed on your van, I thought you had gone off the deep end but I'll be the first to admit you and your van have become an essential part of our investigations."

Ruth beamed. "Thanks Gloria. I love being part of the team."

She gave a toot of the horn before backing onto the road and speeding off into the night.

Lucy wandered over. "She loves her van, but more than that, she loves a good adventure." She turned to face Gloria. "Do you think she'll ever find someone?"

"Maybe." Gloria shrugged. "Too bad we can't find someone who has similar interests in spy equipment."

"I have some ideas," Lucy said. "Let's wait until we finish this case and we can talk about Ruth's love life."

"It's a deal." Gloria grinned. "I'm sorry you didn't get any action tonight."

"It's okay." Lucy shrugged. "The stakeout was a little low key for my tastes. There's always tomorrow."

Lucy hopped into her jeep while Liz and Gloria climbed into the car and drove back to the farm. During the ride, Gloria lectured Liz on safety, to not do anything foolish such as agree to ride in Rex's car and to stay inside the restaurant.

"I've got it," Liz finally said. "You don't give me enough credit. I can handle myself."

"I'm sorry Liz. It's just that sometimes I feel like I'm the big sister," Gloria said. "Despite your aggravating ways, I love you and would feel terrible if something happened tomorrow."

"Aww. I love you too, Gloria." Liz reached over and squeezed her sister's hand. "Don't worry. I'll be careful."

Little did either of them know the plan they had put in place would change drastically overnight.

# Chapter 21

"Gloria? Are you awake?" Gloria groggily lifted her head off the pillow. Someone was pounding on her bedroom door and that someone was Liz.

Paul groaned, rolled over and pulled the covers over his head. "Doesn't she know the roosters haven't even started crowing yet?"

"Sorry dear." Gloria flung the covers back, slid out of bed and shuffled to the door. She opened it far enough so Mally and she could squeeze out and then quietly closed the door behind them.

"I hope the house isn't on fire." Gloria said the first thing that popped into her head.

"No. Nothing that drastic," Liz said in a loud whisper. "I couldn't sleep so I made a cup of coffee and turned the kitchen television on."

"And you were lonely so you thought you'd wake me up to keep you company."

"Of course not. I was watching the local daybreak news. You'll never guess who was found murdered in his driveway last night."

"Who?"

"Rex Wetzel," Liz said. "The police think he stumbled upon a robber when he got home after the party and the thief shot him."

Gloria clutched the front of her robe. Her mind reeled as she followed Liz to the kitchen. "What exactly did Rex say to you when he invited you to lunch today?"

"I told you last night. Rex said he thought he could help hook me up with some great investments," Liz said. "After the news ended, I logged onto the internet and found the news clip. Check it out."

Liz pointed to her laptop, sitting on the kitchen table.

Gloria plopped down on the seat next to her. Liz clicked on a button and a video appeared. She clicked the play button and leaned back so Gloria could get a closer look.

A young female reporter stood in the driveway of a large, brick two-story home. Behind her were several police cars and an SUV with the doors open. There were several police officers milling about.

The reporter explained how a neighbor had called 911 around 11:30 p.m. the previous evening to report gunfire close by. When the police arrived to cruise the neighborhood, they found Rex Wetzel lying in his driveway. He'd been shot several times and one of them had been a shot to the head.

"The police told us they believe Mr. Wetzel may have surprised the robbers and that is when he was shot," the reporter stated.

The camera panned the home as well as the street and then returned to the reporter.

"Wait!" Gloria said. "Rewind the tape."

Liz tapped the keyboard and rewound the footage. "There. Stop the video."

Liz stopped the video. "What am I not seeing?"

"There's a for sale sign in the front yard."

Liz leaned forward. "You're right. I hadn't noticed."

Gloria slid out of the chair. There was some small clue she was missing. What if Rex's killer hadn't been an intruder? She remembered how Dot and Ruth said Rex kept coming out and talking to people in private.

Was Rex the middleman in the Ponzi scheme? Or...what if he was initially involved with the others, decided to cut them out and find his own group of "investors?"

She glanced at the clock. It was only 6:30 on a Monday morning. Ruth would be arriving at the post office soon. "I want to check out Ruth's footage from last night to see if I recognize any of the people Rex met with."

Paul was up by the time Gloria emerged from the bathroom. "I thought I heard you rambling around out here." He eyed her blue jeans and t-shirt. "What's going on?"

Gloria briefly explained what had happened and told him she wanted to check out Ruth's video footage of the people the dead man had privately met with at the party. "I'm not convinced his death was a robbery. It may have been a cover up. Someone was desperate to silence or stop Rex Wetzel."

She promised her husband she wouldn't do anything foolish and then headed to the post office.

Kenny was in the back sorting boxes when Gloria breezed in. "Hi Gloria."

"Hello Kenny. Thanks for covering for Ruth the past couple of days."

Kenny smiled, the dimple in his chin deepening. "No problem. You gals are always good for some entertaining stories."

"Which is why I'm here," Gloria said. "I need to chat with Ruth for a brief moment."

"She's over in the corner," Kenny said. "You can come on back."

Gloria hurried to the back and found Ruth in the corner, surrounded by stacks of mail.

"You're out early this morning," Ruth said.

"Rex Wetzel, the guy you caught on camera coming out of the country club over and over, was found dead in his driveway late last night after the party."

Ruth dropped the stack of mail in her hand. "You're kidding."

"The police suspect he surprised a robber at his home but I think he was targeted. Someone wanted to silence him or stop him." She lowered her voice. "I was hoping I could take a look at the footage from the party to see if I recognize any of the individuals Rex met with."

"Sure," Ruth said as she stepped over a bin brimming with unsorted mail. "Kenny, I'll be right back."

"Yes ma'am." Kenny gave the women a small salute and they headed out the back door of the post office and to Ruth's van.

"Like I said, he came out like clockwork, every ten minutes or so." Ruth started the van and crawled across the seat to the back. She flipped dials on the front of the computer screen and tapped the keys on the keyboard. "I remember the first time I noticed him was at 1800."

"Which is?"

"6:00 o'clock p.m. There." Ruth pointed at the screen.

Gloria squinted her eyes and studied the still video. Sure enough, Rex Wetzel emerged from the clubhouse accompanied by a man and a woman. They stood off to the side, their heads close together. The conversation lasted about three minutes and then they headed back into the building.

"Same thing happened about ten minutes later." Ruth fast-forwarded the clip and then pressed the stop button. "There he is again."

Rex appeared. This time there was a trio of men. They made their way over to the same spot, heads close together and then returned to the party a short time later.

None of the individuals looked familiar. "He does this three times." Ruth fast-forwarded again and again Rex emerged with a small group of people.

"I've got two more recorded." The women watched the other two before Ruth turned the surveillance equipment off.

"None of those people look familiar?" Ruth asked.

"Not a one." Gloria shook her head. "Remember that Nolan Bolton argued with Don not long before his death. This man, Rex, was the first one to mention a get-rich-quick scheme. His house is for sale. My gut tells me he was involved in the scheme, trying to warn others…or maybe he was trying to make his own deals and cut the other investors out." She remembered Liz's comment that Rex had told her he could help her with investments and that she should avoid Ed Shields.

"Or maybe this Rex fella ripped off one of his so-called investors and they took him out," Ruth said.

Gloria climbed out of the van and waited until Ruth shut the engine off, exited the vehicle and locked it. "Don golfed with his buddies every Saturday at one o'clock and always with the same group of people."

She sucked in a breath and closed her eyes. "If you were at the top of a massive money-making scheme, raking in tons of cash, what is one of the first things you would do?"

"Buy more equipment for my van?" Ruth asked.

Gloria opened her eyes and grinned. "Okay, what would most normal people do?"

Ruth shrugged. "Buy a new car."

"Perhaps, but also make sure you've eliminated your competition if you had any." Gloria stomped her foot on the ground. "We don't have a shred of concrete evidence and I know I'm missing something…something important."

She thanked Ruth for showing her the videos and headed to her car. It was time to check in with Margaret.

As she drove to her friend's house, she wondered if Margaret had heard about Rex Wetzel's death.

Margaret's SUV was in the drive. Gloria parked behind her vehicle and hurried to the breezeway door where she rang the bell. She could've sworn she heard a dog barking.

Margaret appeared moments later, holding a small dog.

"What in the world?" Gloria stared at the dog through the screen. "You have a dog."

Margaret shifted the small pooch to her other arm and opened the door. "This is Minnie." She grabbed Minnie's paw and waved it. "Minnie, say hello to Gloria."

Gloria reached out to pat Minnie's head. The small dog started to growl and bared her teeth.

"It takes her a few minutes to warm up to you, but she's a good guard dog. Her bark is definitely bigger than her bite."

Gloria stepped into the breezeway. "I had no idea you liked dogs."

"Me either." Minnie and Margaret climbed the steps and made their way into the kitchen. "I just happened to be driving by *At Your Service* dog training yesterday. I spotted Alice's car so I thought I would pop in to say hello."

"She introduced me to Minnie. I guess someone dropped the dog off outside the kennel and Alice was trying to figure out what to do with her since she can't be trained as a service dog." Margaret set Minnie on the floor and the small dog promptly ran over to Gloria, circled her legs and began barking her head off.

"We were going to stop by your place on the way home but you weren't there," Margaret said. "How did it go last night?"

Gloria answered the question with one of her own. "Have you watched today's local news?"

"No. Why?"

She told her friend about Rex Wetzel's death and briefly explained her suspicions. "I think someone in Don's close clique of golf buddies is the ringleader of the money scheme. Someone found out Rex was trying to warn others and possibly even convince some of their investors to invest with him instead so they decided to take him out."

"Oh my gosh!" Margaret's hand flew to her mouth. "I never cared for Rex. He was a loudmouth, very bossy and opinionated."

"In addition to Don's golf buddies, Club NED, I think one of the ringleaders may be one of the co-owners of the golf course," Gloria said. "I can't remember their names."

"Phil Holt, some man in California. There was a third but I can't remember." Margaret popped out of her chair. "What am I thinking? Don has a file folder with the charter member information. It also lists the owners." She disappeared down the hall, returning moments later waving a manila file folder. "I bet it's in here."

Margaret opened the folder and placed it on the table. The women stood next to each other and studied the papers.

"There." Margaret pointed to the sheet on top. "The joint owners are Phil Holt, Dylan Nestor and Becky Stone."

Margaret shifted her gaze and stared out the kitchen window. "What if Rex Wetzel got caught up in the scheme and attempted to recoup some of his losses by ripping off other people?" she asked softly.

"Or perhaps Rex found out about their money-making scheme, became envious and decided to start his own scam." Gloria rubbed her forehead. "These people...someone is ruining others' lives and they need to be stopped. I still think it's one of Don's golfing partners. There has to be more than one person involved for these types of schemes to work."

Margaret shut the folder and slid it across the table. "What can I do to help?"

"You've already helped immensely," Gloria said. "If you have the time, I would like to pay a quick visit to one of Don's friends. There's also something I need to double check when I get home and then I would like to call Detective Givens. I have an idea."

# Chapter 22

Gloria sat in Detective Given's office and reached for her cell phone. Her fingers trembled as she dialed the number she'd found on the financial information Ed Shields had given her. He didn't answer so she left a brief message, telling him she had finished her review of his investment opportunities and was ready to meet with him.

Detective Givens nodded. "You set the trap. Now we'll have to wait to see if he takes the bait." While they waited to see if he would return Gloria's call, she, along with Paul and Liz, who had accompanied her to the police station, discussed the details of the sting.

The plan was for Gloria to meet Ed Shields at the Snack Shack near the back of the golf course. She would accuse him of running a Ponzi scheme and bilking other club members out of millions of dollars and tell him she had proof.

Her final blow would be when she told him she knew who the other schemers were and then gave him the names, except she wouldn't be bluffing. Gloria was almost 100% certain she knew who the other ringleaders were.

She figured it out after researching the list of suspicious investment companies. One in particular stuck out. It was the luxury resort in "Pelletree," a place that didn't exist.

The final piece of the puzzle had fallen into place when Margaret confirmed the dates Don had taken the money from their retirement, savings and checking accounts. They had all fallen on the same day of the week...Friday, the day before he met his golf partners, Club NED, for their weekly golf game.

Ed Shields called Gloria back within the hour and they agreed to meet at the country club's Snack Shack the next morning at eleven a.m.

Gloria was on pins and needles the rest of the day as she mentally rehearsed how she would tell him she knew he was involved.

Paul attempted to talk her out of it, telling her all the police had to do was bring the suspects in for questioning, to let the professionals handle it but Gloria refused. She'd put a lot of effort into figuring out what had happened and how Don had managed to lose his and Margaret's life savings.

The next morning, Gloria drove Annabelle to the country club. Paul followed behind. Detective Givens had called to let them know they were already on scene and in position.

Gloria rented a cart and headed down the path to the back. When she reached the Snack Shack, she parked off to the side, climbed out of the cart, subconsciously patting the recorder she'd hidden inside her jacket pocket.

Ed was already there waiting, seated at a table near the door. When he spotted Gloria, he sprang from his seat and hurried over to greet her. "You're right on time."

"Thank you for seeing me on such short notice," Gloria said.

"My pleasure. I assume you've decided on your investments. You strike me as an intelligent woman with a keen business savvy many others lack." Ed was laying it on thick.

"I like to think I possess a solid business acumen, which is why I am going to pass on you and your partners' investment offer," she said. "I think it's a scam and a scheme and you've somehow managed to bilk both friends and business acquaintances out of a great deal of money. I plan to report you and your partners to the local authorities."

The look on Ed Shields' face was priceless. "You...you're crazy," he sputtered. "That's ludicrous. You have no proof."

"Oh, but I do," Gloria said. "I think you, along with Becky Stone, one of the co-owners of this fine establishment, cooked up a scheme, a Ponzi scheme to take money from people who trusted you." Gloria tsk-tsked. "Shame on you for doing such a despicable thing."

He opened his mouth but Gloria continued before he had a chance to speak. "The first clue was when Don Hansen cleaned out his bank accounts to pay you. Perhaps the first couple of payments to Don came like clockwork, maybe even more than that. He was doing so well, he decided to invest even more for an even bigger return. By the time he cleaned out his third retirement account, things were starting to go south. You were putting him off on his payments."

Gloria crossed her arms. "Nolan Bolton invested, too. Don tried to warn him and they got into an argument shortly before Don's death. Nolan was still in denial about the scheme. He was still getting those big fat returns and he began trying to convince others to invest with you."

It was time to put a final nail in the coffin. "Margaret and I chatted with Nolan last evening. He finally confessed to taking money from his retirement accounts and giving the money to you. Just like Don, Nolan always took the funds from the accounts on the same day of the week...Friday."

"So?" Ed huffed. "What's that got to do with anything? Besides, it's his word against mine."

"Ah, it has everything to do with it. Don had a standing one o'clock tee time every Saturday. So did Nolan, also a part of *Club NED*. Friday was the day before the men "met" with their financial advisers...you."

She switched tactics as she reached inside her purse, pulled out the financial sheet Shields had sent her and waved it in front of his face. "It's obvious that none of the other investors bothered to research the list of investments you sent me but I did."

She continued. “The luxury resort on the island of Pelletree doesn’t exist. In fact, Pelletree does not exist.”

The color drained from Ed Shields’ face and Gloria thought he was going to pass out. “Follow the money, Ed.” Gloria tapped the side of her forehead. “It’s not that hard. All of this started not long after Becky Stone arrived in Green Springs, joining Montbay Hills Golf & Country club as the third co-owner. That’s when Don started taking money from his and Margaret’s retirement. Same for the Boltons and I’m sure once the investigators start digging around, they’ll find a lot more just like ‘em.”

The expression on Ed’s face changed to a mask of hatred and he took a step toward her. “You meddling dirt bag. If you were smart, you would’ve stayed out of this.” Ed Shields began to growl. “Who do you think you are?”

“That’s enough.” Detective Givens appeared from the back storage room and clamped his hand on Ed's arm. "You're under arrest for fraud, perjury, money laundering and theft, and depending on the outcome into the investigation of Rex Wetzel's death, possibly even murder."

Paul, who had been watching from not far off, strode over. "I just heard they made an arrest up front at the office."

The undercover cops cuffed Ed Shields as they read him his rights.

"You don't know who you're messing with." Shields glared at Gloria. "This ain't over, not by a long shot." The officers led him to a nearby golf cart and drove off.

A burning heat crept up Gloria's neck at Shields' threat. She got the feeling the man held a grudge for a very long time.

"I can't wait to tell Margaret, Liz and the others how Ed nearly confessed to his crime," Gloria said as she climbed into the golf cart parked next to her husband's cart.

Paul leaned over and kissed his wife before sliding behind the wheel of his cart. "Was there ever any doubt?" he teased.

When they reached the front, they parked their golf carts next to the pro shop. Gloria climbed out and took the keys to Paul's cart. "I'll return the keys and cancel the membership now that we've solved the case."

Paul reached out to stop her. "No! I don't think you should. You already paid for the entire month. I've decided I'd like to give it a go."

"Really?" She leaned over and hugged him. "I think you'll like it."

Gloria chattered all the way home about the sting, thrilled to know justice would be served.

The house was strangely quiet when they arrived. "I wonder where Liz wandered off to. I hadn't noticed before, but her car is gone."

Gloria headed to the spare bedroom. The door was wide open. The bed was unmade. Empty food wrappers and trash littered the floor and the top of the dresser but Liz's personal belongings were gone.

"I found this on the counter." Paul stood in the bedroom doorway and held up a key.

Gloria narrowed her eyes. "That's our house key. It looks like Liz took off."

"I hope she's all right," Paul said.

"She's fine," Gloria said. "This is Liz's MO all the way. I wonder if she drove back to Florida."

Just to be safe, Gloria dialed Liz's cell phone and the call went to voice mail. "This is your sister. It appears you've flown the coop. Call me to let me know where you're headed."

"We're empty nesters again," Gloria said as she disconnected the call. "How shall we celebrate?"

"I've been promising to take you to Garfield's for dinner," Paul said as he drew his wife close.

Gloria smiled, a twinkle in her eye. “Hmm. It sounds wonderful but I have an even better idea.”

“Oh you do?” Paul placed a hand behind his wife’s head and drew her close as he gently kissed her lips. “I can’t wait to hear it,” he said before he lowered his head to kiss his wife a second time.

# Chapter 23

"I have a surprise for you," Gloria said as she reached inside her purse.

"For me?" Paul glanced around Garfield's dining room and lowered his voice. "You're pregnant."

Gloria laughed aloud. "Very funny." She reached inside her purse, pulled out a white envelope and slid it across the table.

"What's this?"

"Open it."

Paul opened the envelope and pulled out a *just because I love you* card. Inside the card was a gift certificate for All Seasons Sporting Goods in Green Springs. His eyes widened when he noted the amount. "This is a gift card for five hundred dollars."

"It's the same amount I spent on the golf membership," Gloria said. "I hope you like it."

"I love it, but you shouldn't have," her husband scolded. "I feel even worse now for saying anything since I enjoyed my first attempt at golf."

The couple had visited Montbay Hills earlier in the week for a round of golf. While they were there, they discovered not only had local investigators arrested Ed Shields and Becky Stone but Phil Holt, as well.

The only partner not involved was Dylan Nestor, the silent partner who lived in California. The local news had been covering the ongoing investigation for days now. It seemed not only had Don Hansen and Nolan Bolton been duped, but also several other members of the prestigious country club.

The police were still investigating Rex Wetzel's death as a possible homicide when rumors began to circulate that Rex had originally been in on the scheme with Ed Shields and Becky Stone. When Phil Holt joined the scheme, they cut Rex out. He became angry and decided not only to start his own money scheme but also to sabotage the others by warning potential investors to steer clear.

Gloria had nicknamed the scheme *greed with envy* instead of *green with envy.*

Detective Givens had confirmed Don's death as a suicide and Gloria was saddened to think Don was unable to confess to his wife what he had done so they could work through the financial loss as husband and wife.

Margaret discovered Don had renewed the generous life insurance policy just days before his death and Gloria suspected in his final moments on earth, filled with remorse and regret, he realized he could never recoup the money he'd lost but at least he would not leave his wife penniless.

Paul tucked the gift card in his shirt pocket. "You ever hear from that sister of yours?"

"Yes." Gloria reached for her glass of ice water and took a sip. "She's in Poughkeepsie. She finally confessed the night of the party she'd tracked down Martin's new golf gig in New York and drove there to confront him. She said they patched things up and plan to head back to Florida in another week, when her temporary tenants are scheduled to move out."

"I tried to warn her she was setting herself up for more heartache but she wouldn't listen." Gloria shook her head. "I don't think she'll ever learn."

After dinner, Gloria and Paul wandered down to the water's edge. The lake was as smooth as glass. There was a damp chill in the evening air and Gloria snuggled under Paul's arm. "Poor Margaret. I worry about her and wonder how she's going to adjust to life alone now that Don is gone."

“She has her friends, you and the others,” Paul said. “If not for you, there would be even more sad stories of unsuspecting people being scammed out of their life savings.”

A stiff breeze blew off the lake and Gloria shivered.

“C’mon my dear. It’s time to go home.”

Gloria slipped her hand into her husband’s hand. “Let’s go.”

The end.

The Series Continues... “Garden Girls Cozy Mysteries” Book 16, Coming Soon!

# Get Free Books and More!

Sign up for my Free Cozy Mysteries Newsletter to get free and discounted books, giveaways & soon-to-be-released books!

**hopecallaghan.com/newsletter**

# Meet The Author

Hope Callaghan is an author who loves to write Christian books, especially Christian Mystery and Cozy Mystery books. She has written more than 50 mystery books (and counting) in five series.

Born and raised in a small town in West Michigan, she now lives in Florida with her husband.

She is the proud mother of one daughter and a stepdaughter and stepson. When she's not doing the thing she loves best - writing books - she enjoys cooking, traveling and reading books.

Hope loves to connect with her readers! Connect with her today!

Visit hopecallaghan.com for special offers, free books, and soon-to-be-released books!

**Email: hope@hopecallaghan.com**

**Facebook:**
https://www.facebook.com/hopecallaghanauthor/

# Rose's Black-Eyed Peas Recipe

**Ingredients**:

8 cups water

1 pound dried black-eyed peas (rinsed)

12 ounces ham, diced

6 slices bacon, chopped

4 cloves garlic, diced

1 med. onion, diced

1 bell pepper, diced, (seeded and stemmed)

2 teaspoons ground black pepper

1 teaspoon cayenne pepper

1 teaspoon cumin

Salt to taste

**Directions**:

Pour the water into slow cooker.

Combine black-eyed peas, ham, bacon, garlic, onion, bell pepper, black pepper, cayenne pepper, cumin and salt.  Stir to blend ingredients.

Cover the slow cooker and cook on low for 8-10 hours until the beans are tender.

Serve over bed of white rice with a hot buttered cornbread muffin.

Made in the USA
Coppell, TX
25 July 2023